ANTHONY WENDEL

The
HANDBOOK
for
SURVIVING
a
GIANT MONSTER
ATTACK

"For Rose M. Kish.
An editor, a confidant, a fellow lover of giant monsters, my biggest fan,
and the best grandmother in the world."

Hello, and thank you for purchasing the Handbook for Surviving a Giant Monster Attack. You should congratulate yourself for such willingness to take the time and effort to research such a topic and prepare yourself for that one particular day when you may be attacked by a giant monster. It is this kind of cautious thinking that prevents unnecessary disasters around the house and/or workplace. Give yourself a round of applause...as soon as you put the handbook down first.

It should be brought to your attention that reading this book does not guarantee you will survive the initial giant monster attack unscathed. The fact is, when a giant monster is attacking your city, some forms of collateral damage are likely to be experienced. You might, in the process, suffer the following inadvertent losses:

- Your house

- Your car

- Your family

- That ugly Hawaiian shirt you keep in the back of your closet for that one time that wearing it will be a good idea

Still, with careful preparations and precautions, you will find yourself standing a better chance than that dolt next door who didn't take the time to pick up this book and prepare himself for such a catastrophe. Who knows? It could be that one little piece of information you read from this book that will ensure you're still alive in the smoldering ashes of what used to be your living room. Then you can take the time to have a nice cup of coffee, breathe a sigh of relief, and draft a thank you letter to the author for making sure you were provided with the information that kept you alive.

Rest assured that you're in capable hands. This book has not been thrown together at the last minute, but is instead a carefully thought out and researched piece of preparation equipment. *Through the study of different media-based simulations pieces of media throughout the years and in cross-examination of the techniques that were used in said pieces of media, and taking into account the available technology we have in this day and age, all the different catastrophic possibilities have been taken into account.* This will ensure that no matter what various dinner-interrupting, special event-canceling, and free time-wrecking destroyer of buildings you run into, it will pose little more inconvenience than one feels when receiving a nasty mosquito bite. As long as you're able to stay alive through the ensuing chaos and destruction that is.

Although you yourself are willing to accept the possibility

inevitability of a giant monster attack, you must take into consideration the fact that many people will not share your good-natured intentions. Many will feel that your efforts and energies could be put to better use doing things such as learning a language or keeping in touch with your dear old Aunt Myrtle. (For those of you who do not have an Aunt Myrtle, simply think of a family member you have not talked with for a while.) What these people fail to understand is that what you are trying to accomplish is much more important. In fact, if you are truly prepared for any attack, you'll find yourself being able to use your skills to hopefully save beloved Aunt Myrtle from any unforeseen giant being-related tragedies that might befall her in the near future. One can only hope that once a true creature of terrifying size and scale is on a rampage, your newfound knowledge and preparation will help these naysayers realize would make this book worth the purchasing price. With any luck, you'll be able to learn the proper countermeasures for each individual creature type that might descend upon you and be successful in making a safe escape. Then you can begin the often-overlooked task of beginning the counterattack and eventual destruction of these gigantic living things to ensure that you will be able to return to your regular non-monster related life.

With all that out of the way, let's get started.

Chapter 1:
THE BASICS

The first thing to address when thinking about the survival of yourself and others during any Giant Monster Event (GME), is to first understand the basic preparations and steps that you must take to be able to keep on top of the situation. When dealing with any GME, you have to first understand that it will not simply happen overnight or in the distant future. More often than not, the majority of GMEs occur when you least expect them, giving you little time to react to the events that are unfolding. This means you will not have the time or ability to get the necessary supplies, equipment, and research materials that are necessary to be totally prepared for every GME that befalls you.

Instead, you will discover that you will have to have a much clearer thought process than those around you. You will have to keep calm under pressure and understand that the disaster that you are dealing with is a 300-ton killing machine. With any luck, by the time you've finished reading this book, you will understand the steps that are necessary to take in order to make sure that you and those around you come out on top.

MULTITASKING

Finish reading this Guide all the way to the end. Then read again. Then just to be on the safe side, read it while attempting to run a mile through a very crowded area while simultaneously using your cell phone to look up the weather and traffic reports. Understand that this level of juggling and frustration is only the tip of the iceberg you'll face when dealing with an actual GME. With everything from the running mob of humans to gridlock traffic and the main threat of the monster itself, you'll find yourself having to multitask at a level that you have never even thought about doing. If you're able to do all these things at the same time, you may possess the required level of concentration needed to properly function in any GME.

WARNING SIGNS

One of the best ways to prevent any GME is to be ahead of the curve through researching local events that seem abnormal in nature. Remember that even though these creatures are enormous in nature, they sometimes have the innate ability to go undetected by people around them. It is your job as a concerned human being to make sure that you are ever vigilant to be able to recognize and spot possible pre-GME signs. A mixture of studying the Internet and watching your local morning and evening news will allow you to find news stories that seem out of the ordinary. This will help you to potentially discover a wild monster while it is in a fixed, controllable area. Look for the following types of news reports:

• **Frequently occurring gas explosions.** Due to the highly explosive nature of the material, gas companies around the country make sure to keep up with the highest level of safety codes among any utility provider. If a large amount of incidences of gas explosions occur within a general area over a short period of time, start to investigate. Remember: destruction is the calling card of all giant monsters. You must be able to recognize destruction that is truly accidental from actual GME damage.

• **Multiple missing person's reports in a fixed area.** *It is important to understand is that giant monsters come with the following characteristics: Being loud, being destructive, being a hazard to your livelihood. This means that there will causalities lost with any GME,* and if the monster hasn't made a full appearance, some innocents will be lost without anyone aware of the monster's existence. If multiple missing person reports begin to happen in a fixed area, showing no sign of struggle or reason for disappearance, this can easily be looked upon as the work of a giant monster. Begin to investigate the immediate area of the disappearances during the day when you know that you will be safe, and bring a group of individuals that will be able to help you in your study. If the site of the disappearances exhibits unexplainable destruction of environment or unrecognizable markings of some kind of animal, then you might find yourself in an area that has undergone a low-scale GME. Look for clues that could help you to further your investigation, but be warned that your discovery has placed you square in the monster's territory. Exercise extreme caution while you investigate.

• **Cult activity.** Be aware of the sudden appearance and amassing of a large group of peculiar individuals who keep talking about the appearance or raising of a mysterious being. Be warned that you must not jump to any conclusions when looking at this step. Just because people are talking about weird and mysterious things does not mean that they are indeed attempting the resurrection of some evil creature. They could just be over-zealous comic book fans talking about recent issues. Instead, try accepting some of the pamphlet material that the group is distributing and use it to begin your investigation into the background of the organization. If this group is without any type of written material, try to simply pay close attention and note what they are saying. Using these notes, begin an Internet search to discover if they are worshiping a creature of legend that has a prophecy of resurrecting again. Also, note that usually the raising of these creatures coincides with specific weather, geographical, and astronomical conditions. Check a Farmer's Almanac for any full moons that are scheduled to come in the near future. Most of these monsters have a tendency to rise during full moons. Information on the full dealings with Ancient Creatures will be explained later in this book.

• **Unusual geological/meteorological phenomena.** If it's the middle of summer and you are plagued by a bizarre blizzard when you live in Miami, Florida, or you suddenly experience an unforeseen series of earthquakes in Toledo, Ohio, then it might be safe to say that something is out of the ordinary. These occurrences can be the result of the monster that is either about to emerge or is already on its distorted path. Don't simply shrug off any weird behavior as paranoia; instead, take the time to step back and look at the situation more thoroughly.

Above all, don't jump to any conclusions and try to find evidence of the monster's existence. Hard proof will be necessary to mobilize any type of a counterattack against a rampaging giant monster. You may think you have all the proof you need to prove the monster's existence once it has destroyed a town or two, but people are very skeptical about believing extreme things such as the existence of giant monsters. It will take a large amount of physical proof to get them to understand what is going on. Even then, you might be in trouble getting any type of counterattack going. For now, though, simply do your best to look for any early warning signs and be ready to react when they occur.

SUPPLIES

Unfortunately, there is no universal shopping list when gathering the supplies necessary to cover every conceivable GME that you will face. Many of the supplies obtained for one GME will prove to be useless when facing another. A can of industrial-strength wasp spray will do nothing against a giant python that has the advantage of bobbing and weaving its head so fast that the spray will not be able to keep up. A flamethrower may be useful on some creatures, but it will simply confuse and scare a large, lumbering brontosaurus, causing it to go out of control and trample those in the immediate vicinity.

You will instead have to make a general pile of supplies that will hopefully cover many of the different types of monsters that you will face in a worst-case scenario. Consider keeping a small bag with some of these basic supplies in case a GME does occur:

• **Cell phone:** For communication purposes and alerting the authorities of any possible attack. Ones that have a variety of features (Internet, camera) are especially handy.

• **Dog repellent:** Many of the creatures you'll face will have a sharper sense of hearing. Some stores sell high-frequency animal repelling devices that serve as a portable way to confuse and distract any creature that comes in your immediate vicinity.

• **An Audio Recording Device:** Understand that many may be unsure of what has happened and unable to fathom the events around them. As the GME starts, there is also the possibility that the creature would be unnoticed and its carnage dismissed as some type of freak accident. A recording device will allow you to make proper notes of the GME as it takes place and help in the gathering of information on the giant monster.

• **Camera:** Many of the creatures that you will face will be mysterious or peculiar to those who are unfamiliar in the world of giant monsters. Photographic evidence will help in classifying and studying the creature to optimize the counterattack that you will no doubt be a part of as this is usually how things work out.

• **Water and Light Provisions:** The idea is not to prepare a bag for a full relocation or extended trip, but to put together a field pack that will allow you free movement while providing the basic equipment for staying alive. Consider keeping at least two large bottles of water and portable snacks such as crackers and granola bars to keep yourself alert and on your feet. Do not pack in excess; take just enough to sustain yourself until you can resupply.

• **Flashlight:** There's no telling when the attack will occur, whether in the middle of the day or when it's pitch black outside. Seeing in front of you will be one of the most important aspects you'll need to survive. Make sure to pack a flashlight that is bright enough to see no matter how dark it is and that it is properly stocked up with enough energy to make it through the night on constant use.

• **Flares:** If the creature fears bright light, these will help to keep them at a distance. Also, it's a great back-up plan if you run out of batteries for the flashlight.

• **First Aid Kit:** There is an unthinkable amount of different kinds of hazards that might befall you during your escape. Keeping a small, readily available first aid kit will allow you to patch up any small injuries that might happen. It is also recommended that you take at least a basic first aid class so that you are able to treat any of the hazards or injuries that you receive.

• **A Change of Clothes:** There's no way to know when you'll be able to return to your home or even if you will be able to when this is all over. It's helpful to make sure that you can always change into something clean when you have some downtime in the wake of the destruction.

Please note that the previous list was for dealing with a single GME. In the event of multiple GMEs, you will need a much different set of equipment, and in the result of a full on Giant Monster Invasion (GMI), you'll need an entirely different book to be able to survive. Many of the GMEs discussed in this book are single occurrence in nature. For multiple and frequent occurrences, you will need to prepare on a much grander level and no doubt be required to obtain the help and services of multiple individuals to be able to stay alive.

GENERAL PREPARATION

There are simple steps to take that will help you to be ready for the GME but will not take a huge amount of time out of your schedule. Think of them as little research projects you are doing to ensure you are fully knowledgeable for when the time comes for you to spring into action.

• Finding multiple retreats for when the GME begins. In the broadest sense of monster attacks, you will usually find two major occurrences: either creatures have decided to settle in and destroy a largely populated city or, thanks to the noise from said city, they prefer a more remote location. You need to find a getaway spot that reflects the opposite of your current living situation. If a GME occurs when you live in a large city, then it would probably be a good idea to find a nice, quiet place in the country to get away to in order to escape the ensuing destruction. Usually, you will find that by the time any creature destroys at least one major metropolitan area, someone will take notice and begin some kind of a counterattack. Know that the most important thing is to escape before you deal with any type of counterattack. Please note that you will generally want to put a distance of at least 300 miles between you and the giant monster. Depending on how fast the creature moves will either give you ample time to begin your planning or just enough time to prop-erly think out your next move while huddled over a roadmap to find your next destination. This can also be an effective way for you as an individual to make yourself more familiar with the roads and environment that is around your domicile.

• Watch television specials dealing with and explaining how individuals survived large animal attacks. Though you will not be granted with the ability to get a real-life account of someone actually surviving an attack with a rampaging Tyrannosaurus rex, there are still plenty of large animals that exist in the world that you will be able to study for the purpose of preparing yourself for the appearance of a larger scale creature.

Understand not all of the giant creatures you will face are necessarily 50 feet tall and breathing fire. As an alternative, you may find yourself having to fend off rats that have mutated to more than 10 times their original size. This is still a giant rat you will be dealing with, but it still should not be any bigger than a bull or white rhino. Different programs talking about people who have survived attacks by out-of-control bulls or white rhinos will help you to get a better understanding of how to approach the situation when you are confronted with a creature of equal mass and destructive tendencies. Again, if asked why you are watching these shows and are too embarrassed to admit it's in preparation for a GME, just say you find the topic fascinating and that should stop others from much further questioning.

RECOGNIZING YOU'RE BEING ATTACKED

Some warning signs that you're under a giant monster attack are subtle while others are incredibly obvious. Here are some more common signs that a giant monster is attacking:

• A sudden jolt to the earth followed by amending, unnerving calm followed by more jolts to the earth.

• Every living animal in the general area making a beeline away from your current position.

• That fearful chill running down your spine that something very bad is about to happen.

• There is a 20-story-tall radioactive fire-spewing lizard on your front porch.

Make sure that you don't automatically assume that you're under a giant monster attack by the signs (except for the 20-story radioactive lizard part. That one's undeniable). You don't want to be the only person that's screaming at the top of your lungs while running away at top speed. That just makes you look crazy.

Instead, try doing the following to ensure that you know for a fact that you are in a GME:

• **Check the news.** While people try to hide small-scale disappearances or shrug off mysterious car accidents, the fact is that when a large monster starts attacking, the media will be unable to prevent it from getting out and will be covering it fully. This will offer you assistance in the form of a watchdog that will keep an eye on the creature and report its movements back to you. It should be pretty obvious when there are a series of gas explosions happening simultaneously in the same general area in a limited amount of time that something is probably unusual. That or the gas company in the general area has no idea how to do their job properly. In either case, it would probably be a good idea to stay away from that specific area.

• **Listen for sirens.** Keep your eyes and ears open for police and rescue personnel sirens going off in the distance. If it sounds like 20 cop cars are speeding in a general direction, then there's a good chance that something is up. Also, if you live in an area where air traffic is not that common and suddenly find an entire squadron of Black Hawk helicopters flying overhead, armed to the teeth, then it's safe to say that something is not right.

• **Monitor the flow of people.** Look outside. If a mass group of people are running in a direction at top speed, grabbing only what they can to live and pushing violently to make sure that they make it out of the general vicinity in one piece, then there's a good possibility that something is wrong. That or a bizarre rescheduling has taken place in the Running of the Bulls this year and the location has been moved from Spain to an area not far from your living quarters. Still, the possibility of a marathon you failed to hear about it in the local papers or on the local news is rather high. Be sure to look at the attire that the fleeing individuals are wearing. If they seem to be sporting more dress-down wear with headbands and water bottles at the ready, then it would not be a good idea to begin assuming it's a GME.

Once you know that you are under a giant monster attack, you can begin the process of ensuring that you will live through it. To properly ready yourself for such situations, you must first understand one simple fact: not all giant monsters are the same. There are many different types and styles of giant monsters that have existed in popular media. Taking the proper steps to be able to ready yourself for each specific type of monster attacking your city, town, or state will be discussed later in the book. Instead, we'll start with the general rules to follow when any particular type of giant monster attacks.

Take this opportunity to contact any family members and friends that you know will be affected by the GME. Do your best not to gloat about the fact that you know that you were right and giant monsters do exist. Instead, try and give them tips to make sure that they will be able to get out safely.

CLASSES TO TAKE

There is no way to over-prepare when a giant monster is concerned. Do anything that you think will be able to help you in case one does make an appearance. For starters, consider taking classes that will facilitate you better as the monster starts its advance. These classes will cover a wide variety of topics useful during everyday life, but also essential during a GME.

• **Leadership classes.** Leadership and public speaking classes will help you learn to take charge of a situation when necessary. These classes will also help you in your everyday life to motivate and stimulate your coworkers on the job and at the same time are of critical assistance when a GME takes place. When the monster makes its initial appearance, people will be in a panic, as they will not know how to properly respond to an inexplicable threat of this magnitude. They will be in need of a leader to guide them and make sure that they reach a safe destination. The classes will teach you how to properly gain control of the situation and help the fleeing masses evacuate in a much more organized and safer manner. Any situation can easily be less chaotic as long as a good leader is present.

• **Animal behavior and mentality classes.** Though they're incredibly massive, giant monsters are still essentially large animals. If you have the ability to understand what they are thinking, you can predict their movements, needs and what they're going to do next. This will aid you in your escape, as you will be able to determine where the creature is going to go based on what you know about it. Knowing where it is safe to go and where is off limits will help you plan an escape route that is monster free. An escape route that is without incident is priceless, not only ensuring your safety but the safety of any who are with you.

• **Vehicle maintenance classes.** This is definitely a good skill to have even if there is actually no possibility of a giant monster attacking you in the near future. Vehicle maintenance performed on your own will help save you a lot of money as you will not have to rely on others or have to pay a service charge. It will also become of great value if a GME occurs. If you find yourself trying to get away but run into a complication when your vehicle breaks down, you'll be in serious trouble. But if you understand how the vehicle works and are able to properly fix it, then you'll be better off than individuals who do not have this information.

ESCAPING

As stated previously, the primary worry is escape. Many of the possible GMEs occur when you least expect them and are the least prepared. You will, instead, have to find a means of getting away from the immediate area and find a safer site to assess the situation and properly begin the planning and strategizing necessary to take the giant monster down.

Step 1. Don't panic

Panic is probably the worst thing anyone can do in any situation. It causes an individual to function improperly and lose sight of the goal at hand. The goal in this case: staying alive after a giant monster attack. Let's start with some necessary tasks you can perform to make sure you don't panic. For starters, take a deep breath; a long cleansing breath that can help clear your mind and cause your heart to come down from beating so hard it explodes out of your chest. Try visualizing nice, peaceful scenarios such as waterfalls, meadows, and other calming situations that can make you stop thinking about the fact that a giant monster is coming that could rip you apart or swallow you whole. Keep a calm head, stop yourself from panicking, and progress toward your goal of staying alive during this attack.

Step 2. Grabbing the essentials

Given the fact that you are being attacked by a giant, property-destroying being that leaves nothing alive in its path, your first reaction will be to grab everything humanly possible you want to keep with you. This step is not highly advised at all. You don't want to be one of those people who are so obsessed with physical possessions that they lose sight of the most important goal of staying alive.

Instead, take only the bare necessities and items that are essential for staying alive. Consult the previously mentioned list for some of the items that can help you. You may also have to worry about the possibility of having to exercise personal protection for your safety. Many individuals during the ensuing carnage will not be themselves or in their right minds and may try to lash out in violence in an attempt to save their own lives. Carrying personal protection equipment such as bats and mace just to be on the safe side will help protect yourself from any overseeing violence. Remember that these devices are only for protection and should not be used to harm any individual outside of self-defense.

At the same time, it is highly advised not to use this opportunity to further one's own gain. Don't start charging people for rides or using the confusion to sell devices that you know will not actually help a person, such as a magical rock that will ensure the monster will stop attacking. Also avoid looting or theft from any of the open homes and domiciles of individuals who start to flee from the oncoming destructive force being produced by the GME. You must not be distracted or submit to any unspeakable criminal activity. Your first and foremost priority, again, should be escape.

Step 3. Learning to evade

Running will only get you so far as a means of escape. The ideal method of escape will be through the use of some type of vehicle, but as you start to run, you will encounter one of the biggest obstacles you'll face on top of the giant monster itself: those who are also trying to flee from the monster. The streets are going to be littered with people who are unprepared for such an attack, which means they will be screaming at the top of their lungs and running madly in the opposite direction. Your goal through this confusion will be to find a capable course of escape. In this case, "capable" refers to the idea of being able to bob and weave through the human traffic and make it through successfully.

Probably one of the easiest opportunities to practice this skill would be to attend the madness that is known as Black Friday. Known by many to be the most vicious shopping day of the year, the human traffic that surrounds Black Friday is equivalent to what you'll face in any random, condensed area during a GME. For a real endurance exercise, try waiting in line for hours in front of a store that you know will be highly populated and, when the doors finally open, do your best to maneuver through the traffic to the very back of the store. From there, turn right back around and escape the way you came in. Making your way through this near immovable mob of people is just the type of practice you'll need for the day that a giant monster shows up on your doorstep.

Step 4. Traffic

On top of human traffic, you'll also have to deal with regular traffic. People will be less considerate, to say the least, deciding instead to go as fast as humanly possible and accelerate drastically in a desperate attempt to leave the scene faster. This proves to be one of the most dangerous parts of getting away from the monster other than the monster itself. The possibility of gaining obstacles will be drastically increased by the almost definite fact you will run into bumper-to-bumper traffic, which will eventually cause many people to leave their cars to ensure their own well-being. The best advice one can give in this situation is to be as much a defensive driver as you ever have been. Be sure to check all blind spots thoroughly, watch all your mirrors, and keep an eye on the people in front and back of you, as they will become so zealous that they begin to floor it in a desperate attempt to push your vehicle out of the way to get by. Though a car, truck, or motorcycle is the faster way to get away, it does not mean the danger doesn't decrease, and instead, a new set of hazards will be on the horizon.

Your destination will be up to you, but note that the idea of running to any type of airport and attempting to hop a plane out of the area is not always a possibility. With the many types of monsters attacking, some could possess the ability of flight, which will cause airports to shut down to ensure they are not sending out planes that would be swatted down by an airborne monster. For a much safer destination, see Step 6. (For more information on air traffic, see Planes later in the book)

Step 5. Letting it pass over

One of the more daring options you will be faced with is the possibility of just waiting it out. Depending on the type of monster, this may or may not be a good idea. If you find that the monster rampaging seems to be launching an attack in an almost beeline movement, traveling from one destination to another without any hesitation in its path, then the smartest idea one can have is to just stay at home and hope it doesn't return. Again, depending on the type of monster you are dealing with, you may or may not find this to be the best possible step. Consult later chapters regarding whether or not this step will indeed be effective. You may or may not be setting yourself up for disaster if you continue to remain in place.

Step 6. As you run

As previously mentioned, the most important pieces of equipment to have on hand are a camera and some type of audio-recording device. Many of the creatures involved in the GME will be unknown and will not have been previously documented by science. This means that any information obtained on the subject will be helpful in order to properly stage a counter-of-fensive against the creature. The camera will allow you to take pictures to give those who've not yet seen the creature an idea of what they are dealing with, while the recording device will be used to take any notes as you escape the scene. Try to look for anything you think might be useful when dealing with the creature. Characteristics such as how fast it moves, what type of offensive abilities it possesses, any unique observations about its build or any glaring physical weaknesses should be recorded.

Does the creature only appear at night? It could mean that it's nocturnal, which means it does not like bright lights. Armed Forces personnel will be able to use this information to stage a counterattack by arming themselves with flash bang grenades that they know will cause the creature to become confused and disoriented. This is all thanks to the field reports that you took and documented while on the run from the creature. Just because the creature is bigger than you, do not automatically assume that you are hopeless against it. Many times, the creatures will not possess the ability to achieve rational thoughts, which will give us targets of its devastating terror the advantage we need to control, subdue, and/or destroy it.

Step 7. Finding assistance

One of the small comforts that comes with a GME is the idea that you will have some type of backup in the situation. Unlike other monster attacks such as vampires or werewolves, a giant monster has such a destructive scale that it is very easy to notice. This will mean more individuals will know of the creature's existence than just you. This will result in some type of government assistance such as local emergency services and military that will eventually appear on the scene to help you. Still, don't rely too heavily on their appearance until you are able to find them in the ensuing chaos.

Know the lay of the land. In any situation, it is important to note the various resources that are on hand. You should note the closest fire department, hospital, and police station in your general area. At the same time, it's helpful to have backup lo-cations of emergency aid just in case the monster is coming in the direction of your first choice. Remember, if the monster's coming, that probably means what was in that direction is no longer there.

The groups that will no doubt have the tools and resources necessary to take out these various types of behemoths are the different branches of the armed forces. Whether it is the Army, Navy, or Air Force, it is important to note the various armed services locations that are closest to you. Not that getting these locations will ensure your safety, but they will host some of the most heavily trained and armed people ready to take out any large creature that is on a destructive warpath. Get to them and stay safe.

Step 8. When to fight back

Hopefully now you've gotten away.

Let's run a check, shall we?

Are you alive?

Are members of your party alive?

Are you all angry and ready to kick some giant monster butt?

Then it's time to go on the offensive. Although many times its best just to leave this type of situation to the various armed forces, there's always the few exceptions where you will need to help out. There will always be the possibility that you will be faced with a situation where you are the only individual that has the opportunity to stop the giant creature from being able to rear its ugly head again. As stated previously, many of the steps listed here may have to be modified depending on the different types of monsters that you encounter. The same can be said then for the idea of staging a counterattack. You'll need to know what you're going up against if you have any hope of successfully destroying that giant nuisance.

Also, keep in mind that you need to obtain some kind of safe zone for everyone in your party. You can't just make it to safety on your own and think that it's time to go on the offensive. Taking down the monster will not be a one-man show despite what you envision or have seen in movies. You will need backup and lots of it.

Step 9. Starting the counterattack

There are few conceivable GMEs that would not require you to seek the armed services in assisting you with mounting some type of counter-offensive. These services will provide you with the necessary equipment you'll need including monitoring devices, tracking equipment, weapons, and the provisions necessary to be able to survive any GME. Consult a later chapter in this novel for more information on beginning your counterattack.

AREAS OF
ESCAPE

Being aware of your surrounding area will be necessary if you hope to keep from sealing your own fate by choosing a dead end. You don't want to escape to an area that serves to heighten the movement or abilities of the monster that is attacking you. Instead, you will want to try moving to an area that provides you an advantage hindering the advance of the creature and giving you more time to escape to safety. Here are some of the more common locations to consider when on the run.

• **Forests:** The trees of a thick forest may be able to aid you when you're trying to escape the giant monster's view on foot. If the monster is less than 50 feet tall, you will be able to use the thick forest as an obstacle. That will take the creature a long time to maneuver through. More than likely, despite its large destructive prowess, it will find it difficult to push over trees with roots that lie deep in the earth. This means that the creature will have to plow down each tree that comes in its path to stay on your trail. The additional danger presented with this idea, though, is that there is always the possibility that the monster will cause a tree to collapse and fall on top of you. Consider weaving through the trees instead of running in a straight line. This will help hinder the monster's view of you, increasing the chances that it will lose interest and find another target or snack.

Please note that any large monster over 50 feet will no doubt have the power necessary to topple trees and add to the possibility of your being crushed underneath fallen trees by causing multiple to fall over at once. Also, if the creature is large but at the same time slender and agile, it will move through the forest with ease, and you will again find yourself at a disadvantage. Make sure to do your best to assess the situation before acting irrationally and causing yourself to become cornered.

• **Bodies of water:** If you know for a fact that the giant monster pursuing you is 100% land-based and does not possess any desire to swim, then the idea of some type of water escape becomes favorable. You can use a local ship to escape the immediate area, leaving the pursuing monster on land, yelling angrily as you make your way out to sea. Before you get on the vessel, it will be helpful to have some kind of a destination when you leave the shore. You can't just hang out in the middle of a large lake and hope that the creature on the shore will eventually lose interest in you.

Make sure to take into account the physical ability of the creature. You don't want to make it out to sea and realize just how far it can jump. If you thought a 40-ton monster was scary when it was simply charging at you, think what type of problems will occur if it somehow finds a way to jump into the air and come crashing down on top of you.

• **Cities:** If the creature is totally fixated on you, one of the better ideas is to go through a city. However, while you will be able to use the large buildings and structures to your advantage to slow down the creature, confuse it, and hopefully get it trapped underneath a collapsing building, you do run the risk of endangering many people with the destruction caused by having it in the area. Consider using this as a last ditch effort.

The only possibility for survival is to run into an office building and have the creature mindlessly destroy some of the pillars which hold up the entire building, causing the entire structure to fall down around it. Try to at least have the humanity and decent courtesy about you to attempt to find a building that is closed or has been evacuated. This is highly risky to your well-being as it will be hard to get out without any injury. This is why you will want to use this as one of your last possible terrains to escape to.

• **Plains:** This could very well be one of the worst areas to run to when fleeing a monster attack. Open plains offer absolutely no cover or advantage when in the middle of your escape. There is nothing to hide your presence or you provide any type of obstacle to hinder the monster that is chasing you. The only conceivable reason you would run toward a field at all is because you are in peak physical condition, and you foolishly believe that you stand a chance of outrunning the creature. Know that on foot you stand little to no chance of being able to outrun the majority of the giant creatures that exist. So don't try it. Still, with the right type of off-road vehicle, you might be able to use the plain to achieve top speed and increase your chance of getting away from the creature.

• **Tundra:** If you are in tundra or any snow-laden area, it is in your best interest to escape from the area immediately. For the most part, creatures usually have a way of waking up in an environment that they are able to freely maneuver through. Even when properly equipped with heavy clothing or specialized vehicles, humans for the most part have the inability to escape at high speed in heavy snow areas. Do your best to try and find some kind of snowmobile and use it to escape to a higher climate area that will no doubt be uncomfortable to the creature, causing it pain and giving you the upper hand in the situation.

At the same time, this area could be used as a trap against the creature. If the creature starts in a drier area and continues to pursue through the harsh, bitter, cold weather of tundra, it may become sluggish and unable to keep up with the freezing cold around it. With the movement now controlled, you will have obtained the advantage you can use to defeat the creature. Be sure to wrap yourself in the appropriate clothing to keep out the cold, or you'll find yourself in no better condition than the monster that blindly made its way into the frozen area.

• **Farms:** This is not so much a trap as it is a distraction. If you know a farm in the area that has constant activity, then you have the option of luring the creature there and hoping that farm's products will take the creature's attention off of you. If the creature is carnivorous in nature, a dairy farm could allow it to eat its fill of the local cattle. If it is an herbivore, you might be able to lure it into a field and lay low while it feeds. The quiet atmosphere along with the bountiful dinner will allow the creature to calm down, find satisfaction, and stop wanting to chase after you. Don't feel bad about destroying the farmer's crops as the government will no doubt try and reimburse the farmers for their wares in gratitude for helping to tame the wild beast.

• **Deserts:** Similar to the tundra, you will be at an advantage and disadvantage. Your goal will be to lure the creature into a desert area that it is unfamiliar with and use the shifting sands to hinder the creature's movements and slow its advance. Of course, a creature that originally came from the desert will no doubt be able to move at a speed much faster than you could on foot or in a vehicle specially designed to weather the harsh desert conditions. Again, exercise extreme caution and know what you are getting yourself into before it's too late.

METHODS OF ESCAPE

Selecting the right vehicle will be critical when escaping. Depending on the situation, where you are, and what type of monster you are going against, your escape vehicle of choice could either spell disaster or provide you with just the amount of mobility necessary to escape the area and make it to safety.

Cars: As one of the most common forms of transportation in the world today, this will no doubt be the first choice you'll consider when thinking about escape. This will allow you to escape much faster than you could on foot, but please keep in mind that you need to use the right kind of car to ensure that you make it out safely. A car that might be able to get you from point A to point B normally might not be the best idea when attempting to escape from a rampaging monster. There are some simple guidelines to follow when choosing the right car to use for your getaway.

1. The right paint job could make or break your escape. All of these creatures have different types of vision. It they have vision that is attracted to colors, the hot red paint job that you just got for your car might cause it to stand out and draw the wrong attention. You want to be able to get away without drawing any attention to yourself, and driving a vehicle with a color that keeps the monster on you like ants to sugar is definitely a bad idea. Keep this in mind if you have the luxury of choosing what type or color of a getaway vehicle to use.

2. Whisper quiet is your friend. As stated with the first point, you want to make sure not to draw any unnecessary attention to yourself. This means that you don't want to choose a vehicle that runs so loudly that it annoys the creature and make it wish for your utter destruction. A nice, quiet sedan or midsize car is perfect for having a good deal of speed but at the same time possessing an engine that allows you to go unnoticed by the monster and get away that much easier.

Trucks: Usually built for being able to withstand some of the harsher conditions, a truck or SUV allows the driver the option of going off-road if needed and take a more scenic path in their escape. At the same time, these vehicles come with the disadvantage of not getting up to speed as easily as smaller cars. If given the option when selecting the escape vehicle, try and briefly plan ahead on the route you will be using to get away. If you can use a path that is more off-road, then take the truck. But if you find yourself going through more straight-aways and need speed, then it would be a better idea to look elsewhere.

1. Size does matter. As previously noted, some of the giant monsters you will find will only be enlarged versions of rather tiny things, such as ants the size of cows or mantises as big as elephants. If you find that you have at your disposal a large and reinforced truck that will allow you to smash into these enlarged versions, then by all means do so. Yes you may have to worry about wrecking and damaging the truck, but at the same time, if you succeed in ridding yourself of the opposing giant monster with a loss of only a vehicle, you should consider yourself very lucky. Normally, an enlarged ant or mantis will be able to move more freely than some of the bulkier, skyscraper-toppling monsters in the world. This means if you find yourself with the ability to destroy the monster without any large-scale planning, then it would probably be a good idea to do so. One wrecked vehicle is a much better idea than watching the creature climb in and devour a busload of orphans being watched by nuns. Keep in mind, you need to observe the situation and reflect on whether smashing into the creature will do any harm. You don't want to harm your vehicle or yourself needlessly.

Motorcycles: If you refer back to step 4, you'll notice that one of the bigger problems you will face in your escape will be the gridlock from traffic that is created from the mass number of individuals trying to escape the GME. In this gridlock, you'll find small pockets of openings that a skilled and careful driver will be able to use to move ahead of the pack with a small vehicle. This is where the motorcycle comes into play, which will allow its operator the ability to get ahead of the curve farther than some of the wider and cumbersome vehicles such as vans and SUVs.

1. Again, watch the noise. Many people prefer to customize their motorcycles with pipes that cause them to make more noise than their stock options. Though this might be a good idea when riding in a large group on a weekend drive, it will instead be very hazardous during a GME. An extremely loud and deafening sound will instead draw attention to your vehicle and may even annoy the creature that is pursuing you. Try to instead select a cycle that is small and allows you to get up to speed rapidly.

2. A man-made obstacle course. Understand that the newly formed obstacle course will not be as easy to maneuver through as previously stated. Although there will be those who will try to cling to their vehicle and not want to leave it under any circumstances, there will be those that upon seeing the unmoving traffic will instead opt to leave their vehicle and get ahead on foot. This will create the problem of open doors and pedestrians blocking the very narrow path that you are trying to use. Depending on when and how they appear, you might cause unintended harm to yourself or others. Make sure that you have complete control and are skilled in operating your cycle before you attempt to maneuver through the gridlock.

Planes: The easiest way to get around the traffic on the ground is to simply not deal with it at all. If you have the ability to make it to an airfield and use some type of plane to get away, then by all means use it. You will be able to not only avoid having to maneuver through obstacles, but will be blessed with the luxury of escaping into a higher altitude that is out of reach of some giant monsters. Still, this option is not without its drawbacks, and you'll find yourself having to ask some important questions before considering flight a possible variable.

1. Can you really fly a plane? Not every plane that you come across will be readily staffed with individuals able to man the vehicle and assist in your escape. Instead, you may find yourself left with the option of taking out a much smaller plane that would only hold a few people. The real question you will need to ask yourself is: once you have the option of using this small plane to make your escape, will you be able to? Do you have any experience in flying? Have you ever taken a course or spent any time in a simulator? Will you be able to tell the speedometer from the altimeter? If you have absolutely no experience in piloting a vehicle such as this, then it will do you no good. Getting in it will serve no purpose but to injure yourself and those around you; the last thing you want to do is add anymore carnage to the GME taking place. If by chance you are a trained pilot, then by all means, find a local airstrip and use a plane to get away. Though it is ill-advised that you steal a plane, understand that any GME will be looked upon as an extenuating circumstance. This means that any rational and clear-thinking individual will probably exonerate you from any infraction against the law that might occur during a GME.

2. What are you fleeing from? Understand that there are some circumstances where the use of the plane will not be the best available option. First, what if the giant monster in question possesses the ability of flight? If it does, you will be in its home territory and at a high disadvantage. More often than not, the creature will simply be able to maneuver much more swiftly than you will and thereby be able to pass your vehicle, causing it to go out of control by the sheer force of a larger object passing by so closely. You also run the risk of the monster looking at you as if you were a threat or merely some type of bug to be swatted, which will make it slam into you and destroy your vehicle. Unless you are in a fighter plane, it is probably not a good idea to challenge the creature to a fight in the air. Also, if you are in a fighter craft, then you are no doubt in the armed services and will be briefed with information by experts who will offer you greater options and advice than what is found in this book.

A rare but not unseen problem to consider is the possibility that the giant monster has the ability to fire some type of projectile as an offensive measure. This will not only increase the amount of destruction that will occur in the GME, but also take away your ability to escape into the air. The idea of escaping to the air centers on the idea that you are facing some type of land-based creature that will no longer become a threat once you reach higher altitudes. Unfortunately, if you find yourself having to contend with a creature that possesses the ability to shoot spikes at the speed of a tank's cannon, then getting into a plane will be a bad idea. The creature will still look upon you as an annoyance and will attempt to fire one of its spikes to destroy your plane. However, if its attack is limited to only a slightly extended area and you are able to quickly climb to a height outside of its range, by all means, stick with the idea of using a plane as your method of escape.

Boats: Any good water-based escape will be totally meaningless if you do not have a boat. Sure, there is a possibility that when you make it to the water, you will be able to swim out far enough that the creature will not consider you worth the trouble, but this will probably not be the case. Instead, what you'll find is that the body of water will be more like a wading pool or small puddle for the monster to traverse. This limits the idea of using water as a means of escape unless you are absolutely sure that you will have a boat or some other type of aquatic vehicle at your disposal. Do your best to think ahead and know if you will actually have this option.

1. Avoid size and go with speed. Many GMEs will inspire individuals to act on the grounds of nobility and honor. The hardship caused by any of these events will motivate people to try and save as many others from harm as humanly possible. Though it is recommended that you do everything in your power to save lives, you must understand that you will not be able to save everyone. This will become overwhelmingly apparent when you try to escape via water. One of your first intentions, no doubt, will be to try and use a vehicle that can carry as large a number of people as possible, hoping you will be able to take many survivors away from danger. Understand that, although a noble goal, it might do more harm than good. A larger vehicle is a larger target, and the majority of these simpleminded creatures will be easily threatened by them and may attempt to mount some type of attack by lunging at it. This means that a large vessel containing a large number of frightened survivors could very well become a buffet for the creature to gorge itself on. Also realize that a bigger vehicle will take longer to get up to speed and will thereby slow down your escape. A better idea is to try and use a smaller and faster craft that will allow you to travel at a greater distance in a shorter amount of time, placing a larger gap between you and the creature.

Bikes, Skateboards: Though small and only powered by the amount of force you are physically able to summon at the time, bikes and skateboards do offer some type of help in many GMEs that can occur. Much like the previously mentioned motorcycle, these items will allow you to maneuver through traffic much better than those around you. A bike will allow you to gain more distance than you would simply being on foot and an individual possessing a great deal of skateboarding skill will be able to move through areas much quicker than the average runner. It is important to point out, however, that these vehicles are primarily for obtaining an advantage when dealing with human traffic. You will inevitably want to find some type of motorized vehicle to upgrade to in the hopes of ensuring a successful retreat.

Construction Equipment: Though not as much for a means of escape as a tool of defense, construction equipment can serve to help you thwart and dispose of a creature that is on the attack. Through the use of construction equipment, you will be able to once again, depending on the size of the creature, attack and subdue it. If you are under the attack of a 30-foot mutated mole, for example, you may be able to use a bulldozer to hold the creature back and allow those around you an ample amount of time to escape the area. In fact, if you are able to organize a fleet of bulldozers, you might find yourself able to take on an entire horde of enlarged creatures seeking the destruction of mankind.

1. Training is key. Once again, as similarly mentioned with plane operation, you will need special training when dealing with construction equipment. Sure, many forms of media insist that you will be able to simply hop into any piece of construction equipment and use it to plow down the mutated mole that keeps appearing all over town and dragging people down into its lair, but this is definitely not the case. You will instead find yourself unable to properly maneuver the vehicle and may result in causing more harm than good; potentially even causing more destruction than the monster in question. Only get behind the wheel of construction equipment if you know how to operate it to a degree that you are able to stop it in the event that it goes out of control or is about to risk the health and well-being of others. The idea of using the equipment is to help others and not hurt them.

WEAPONS

When fighting off the attack of a giant monster, you'll want to make sure that you use the proper weapons to ensure the most effective amount of damage necessary to defeat the creature. If you are too poorly armed, you will find that the creature will simply be annoyed by your attack which will cause it to become enraged and wish for your destruction. Keep in mind that you will want to do the most amount of damage possible to ensure that the creature is indeed taken care of properly.

Shotguns/Handguns: To have any hope of defending yourself, you'll want to be armed with weapons that cause large amounts of damage but will not hinder you from walking or, in worse case scenarios, running. This means that weapons such as high-powered shotguns or the .44 magnum will have enough kick behind them to be able to penetrate the thick skin of the giant monster. Stay away from low-power guns such as the 9 mm, as it will not get the necessary results that you were hoping for, and would more likely aggravate the monster.

Ammunition: Just because you have a high-powered gun doesn't mean that you have the right ammunition. For example, a shotgun loaded with rock salt or buckshot will do nothing to a large creature and will instead give you an undeserved sense of confidence. If you have the option, pick up armor-piercing rounds or even explosive rounds, as they will be able to penetrate the creature. Make sure that you know the ammo you carry, what you have loaded into your gun, and how much damage you will be able to do before you take the first shot.

Rockets: Rockets are essential for dealing with large targets as they offer the greatest amount of destructive power while still possessing mobility. A rocket that hits its mark can, depending on the creature, cause enough damage to destroy it instantly. Though this is a key weapon to have at your disposal in a GME, it is not without its setbacks. Most rocket launchers are made primarily to be one-shot, one-kill weapons. This means that if you are unfortunate enough to miss with your first shot, you may find yourself at a disadvantage. Make absolutely sure the shot you are about to take is going to hit or you will risk the possibility of leaving yourself completely vulnerable.

Explosives: If you wish to do extensive amounts of damage, you want to make sure to consider the possibility of using high explosives. Explosives lack the option of accessibility, as you are usually required to have both the experience in knowing how to set the charges and enough time to be able to set them up to explode properly. This means that you'll have to set some type of a trap in an area where explosives have already been placed and then find a way to lure the creature over to that general area. Once it is close enough, you may detonate the explosives and destroy the creature. Make sure that you know what you are doing when setting up these explosives, as you do not want to accidentally have them explode on you, causing irreplaceable damages to yourself or others.

Combination guns: Through advancements in modern warfare, weapons that allow for different situations have become available. Weapons such as machine guns armed with grenade launchers give you the option of wielding two different styles of weapons at the same time. Having access to these guns allows you to confuse the creature by not giving it the option of predicting what type of fire is coming next. An advantage, no matter how small, is still an advantage when fighting against any giant monster.

CLEAR
THINKING

Keep in mind above all else that one of the most important policies to practice and exercise during any GME is keeping calm and rational thought. Many of those around you will not be blessed with the same clear thought process that you will be blessed with at the time of the GME. It will be up to you to take a deep breath, analyze the situation, and remember the lessons you've memorized from this book. From there, you'll be able to understand, plan, and work toward being able to properly escape from the situation so that you will be able to take part in the inevitable counterattack to stop the scourge that is ruining the lives of so many individuals locally and across the world.

Now that you understand some of the basics of preparation and escape, it's time to study some of the creatures that you will meet face-to-face. Memorizing all the data in this book is essential to prepare yourself for whatever type of monster you will encounter.

Chapter 2:
THE DIFFERENT TYPES OF MONSTERS

Just like there are many different types of apples or numerous species of cats, there are equally a multitude of monsters to destroy cities and homes. Although there is a better chance of being attacked by some more than others depending on many factors, including your geographical location and what season of the year it is, a broad and extensive knowledge of every possible monster class will allow you the opportunity to ensure that no matter what type of creature is on the loose, tearing apart your area, you will know the proper way to escape and what to do when the time comes to stage a counterattack.

ATOMIC

About: Soon after the bombing of the Japanese city of Hiroshima, mankind entered into the atomic age. Through the media of literature and cinema, humans were able to gain perspective on what kind of abilities nuclear power had, giving birth to the idea that it could spawn monsters. Some of the best monsters of fiction have been created this way. The original idea was that the radiation caused the creature to mutate, increasing its size to exponential proportions. Although this might have been a good idea in the past, humans know better now. Studies into the effects of radiation have shown that a creature that undergoes a mutation experiences a breakdown in its genetic code. This means that creatures exposed to radiation have the tendency of becoming disfigured and sometimes even bear absolutely no resemblance to their original form.

Warnings: When dealing with a creature that has been mutated thanks to nuclear or atomic radiation, one the biggest problems you will face is the possibility of excessive radiation from any type of initial contact with the creature. Excessive exposure to the radiation has caused the creature to absorb so much it actually becomes immune to the effects. Unfortunately, this has a way of causing the creature to emit a level of radiation. This will result in anyone who has too much exposure to the creature to eventually develop severe medical problems. If you are blessed with the option of obtaining a hazmat suit, it would be beneficial to get one, especially if you have any type of intention to investigate the area the creature originally rampaged through. This will prevent you from experiencing unfortunate side effects from exposure.

Additionally, please note that science has denounced the idea of radioactive exposure causing magical powers such as breathing fire or shooting laser beams from the eyes. Though the idea seems laughable now that we know the full extent of what exposure to nuclear materials can really result in, it is still a recommended safety precaution to treat the creature as if it does possess some type of mystical destructive power. Until you are blessed with the information to correct yourself and understand the full extent of what you are dealing with, prepare for a worst-case scenario when dealing with these creatures. You don't want to start a counterattack only to discover that the monster has been hiding an ability which causes more than half of your forces to be totally wiped out.

Recommendation for Escape (RFE): Despite being horribly mutated by nuclear energy, the fact of the matter is that the creature will still maintain the same characteristics it had before it found itself having 10 times its body mass. This means for the most part that it will appear from and disappear to its original habitat at the end of the day. The trick is simply finding out where its habitat is located. Understand that since it did suffer a blast from a nuclear test, there are few areas that fit the bill for this kind of circumstance. Nuclear bombs are usually tested on either areas of empty desert which receive absolutely no human traffic or deserted islands. This usually means that the creature will appear from a desert area or from the ocean. The most logical step to take when dealing with one coming from the desert is to head into the mountains. Since it came for the desert before its mutation, it was obviously a type of creature that prefers to be in a drier humid climate. This means that escape into the higher elevations of the mountains is a much safer bet, as the creature will no doubt not want to venture too high and risk being affected by the chilling climate that is around it.

The same thought process must be applied to the nuclear creature coming from the ocean, just on a different level. Since it is coming from the ocean, this means that before its mutation it possessed some type of amphibious qualities. Even though its body is now fitted to withstand some of the harsher land climates, it may only be able to stay on land for so long. Eventually, it will need to return to the water in hopes of re-hydrating its body and rest from the destruction it has inflicted while on land.

Avoid: Although the idea of fighting fire with fire (or in this case nuclear fire) might arise, this route must be avoided at all costs. Don't fire a nuclear bomb at a nuclear creature. Even though the destruction will be incredible, it will be a very bad idea to try and jump to some of the more extreme ideas when a giant monster attacks. One of the most extreme solutions we have in this age is the "nuclear option" of using a radioactive bomb to finish things off because of the amount of danger to people in and around the target. An even worse scenario is that the creature mutates again and becomes even stronger.

Counterattack: With any good counterattack, you want to look for your opponent's weakness and attempt to exploit it. Again, remember that despite its size and mutation, the creature is one of habit. It is this habit that will lead to its eventual destruction.

In the case of a desert creature, you should be able to discover that it has some type of lair such as cave that it uses to sleep and get out of the hot desert sun. Since it is already in an enclosed area, the most logical course of action would be to find a way to keep it trapped in there permanently. In other words, simply bury it. Either gather a small team of properly equipped (don't forget the radiation suits) individuals armed with demolition materials to blow up the wall and ceiling of the lair, causing a cave-in, or simply get the armed forces to arrange an effective airstrike against the area and cause a cave-in from the outside. The basic idea is that, despite the monster's size, it will be unable to survive the weight of all the rocks crashing down upon it.

The ocean mutant, on the other hand, poses a much more complicating situation. Once it escapes into the sea, it will be able to move at a speed and agility that even the most advanced submarines will find difficult to match. This means that not only will keeping up with the monster be difficult, but tracking it will be just as tricky. There is no way to monitor the entire ocean when in pursuit of the creature. Instead, a strategic operation will have to take place involving multiple water-based crafts that can work in tandem to set up a monitoring perimeter. Together, they will be able to triangulate the creature's location and eventually follow it back to its lair. Once its lair has been discovered, the most effective way to get rid of it is to use depth charges on the immediate area until you're absolutely sure the creature has been eradicated. Although the most impulsive step will be to simply send the team down to confirm that the creature is dead, this might be a poor idea. Instead, once the creature's heartbeat has disappeared from sonar, continue monitoring for a period of time that will give you the option of being able to resume the dropping of depth charges to try to eradicate the creature again. After a period of 12 hours has passed, and it seems to still remain motionless, you may begin your investigation. However, it would still be of best interest to send down an unmanned probe first to check the area before sending down a manned vessel that could be lost.

SPACE

About: Major misconceptions that people have when thinking about aliens from another planet is that that they will simply be scrawny, gray, large-eyed beings with an intent to probe humans for some type of case study. This is not always the case, as there are many aliens who will look upon humanity as a nuisance and attempt to do everything in their power to try and eradicate us so that they can conquer the earth for their own intentions. The "everything in their power" we are going to focus on today is the possibility that these conquerors will have some type of giant monster at their disposal they will use to wipe the human race out. Please note that when dealing with this type of invasion, you will not only have to worry about attacks from the creature, but also the aliens' vehicles. Advice on having to stop a flying saucer that is armed with death rays is better handled by another guide, however. For now, we will concentrate on the idea that the aliens have unleashed some type of alien creature that they will use to destroy the entire populace.

Warnings: Although any being that is giant in nature has the potential of being deadly, creatures from space seem to stand out above the rest. This comes from their origin. Even creatures from space that are not being controlled by some type of alien overlord still tend to be more advanced than anything we have seen on earth. This is backed up by the information from long-range satellite photos that show many other planets unable to support any type of life that we know of. This means that wherever the creature comes from it, must be an environment that is far harsher than the earth for the most part. The body structure for the creature that appears will no doubt be one that is resilient to extreme temperatures and does not necessarily have to rely on the air in our atmosphere to breathe. In fact, depending on how serious the attack is, the creature could very well be designed to simply detonate and destroy all life in the vicinity. Keep this in mind when the monster first appears and accept that, without the proper research and study to justify how to properly take down the creature, you risk not only harming yourself but others by acting rashly.

RFE: In an attempt to conquer the better part of the world, the first targets that the aliens will choose will be places of political and strategic value. This means that capital cities or places with a large mass of people will be the first attacked. As stated earlier, you want to have a place you can run to in the country if a monster attacks the city first. With the probability being high that the creature will possess some type of projectile weapon, you will want to stay away from any type of air traffic as a means of escape. Any air vehicles will be easily shot down by the creature or by one of the alien crafts that are in the area. Try to stay in cars, trucks, or even moving on foot as the creature will be concerned with destroying buildings more than it will be with you as an individual. Take this opportunity of not being of concern to make it to the country.

Avoid: It is ill-advised to send the creature back from whence it came. Sure, it seems like the most logical idea to simply find a way to trap the creature back in the vehicle that brought it here in the first place, but this idea is not without its share of problems. For starters, it will not be as easy as pushing it back inside its pod (or whatever type of spaceship it arrived in), pressing a button, and watching it fly back into the stratosphere. Keep in mind that you have absolutely no idea how the alien technology works, and there is an even greater possibility that you will not even be able to understand the language that they use. Finding the right button or sequence of buttons to get the ship to leave is a near impossible task. With time being one of the biggest factors, as there is no telling when the beast will become unmanageable, your actions must instead be quick and effective. You will not have time to translate or read an alien instruction manual to get the pod working.

The other point to remember is the possibility that there is no pod to begin with; that the creature came from some kind of meteorite. It will not be uncommon for aliens to disguise the egg of a giant monster in a meteor and send it hurtling toward the earth, allowing it to hatch and grow into the destroyer they need to deal with the nuisance of humanity. There will be no possible way to shove the creature back into its broken egg or crashed meteor in hopes of using either as a way of ridding yourself from this menace from space. Seek other ways of dealing with the problem, as the creature is already here and you will have no choice but to defeat it.

Also take note to resist any attempts by you or those in your group to simply give up and worship the aliens in their grand conquest. Yes, there may be moments when it seems like all hope has run out as the alien succeeds in wiping out a few major cities, but that does not mean it is time to give up. Do your best to insist that you will be able to find some way of counterattack to help motivate your group to stay positive.

Counterattack: If the aliens are smart—and there's a pretty good chance of that considering they are now mounting a worldwide attack on the entire planet—then they will also be cautious. This means they more than likely have a means of controlling the giant monster to use its destructive force effectively, and perhaps also some type of emergency stop to cease the creature's movements, if need be. This giant monster control system is what you'll need to focus on when beginning your counterattack. Scientists specially trained in the field of sound and frequency will need to study the area around the attacking creature to try and locate some type of signal that is being used to manipulate its movements. Once you are able to isolate, copy, and analyze the signal, you will be able to use it to take control of the monster and have it turn on its former masters. Be warned: although the creature is now under your control, you will still have to deal with the problem of what to do with it now that it's here to stay. At least with the destruction of the aliens, you will not have to worry about it doing any more damage.

PRODUCT OF
HARRYHAUSEN
LABS

SCIENCE

About: Much like the previously mentioned atomic and nuclear monsters, science has a way of creating problems by diving into and conducting experiments that sometimes cause disastrous results. Two of the biggest areas of science that pose the most immediate threat are the fields of genetic manipulation and technology.

In the field of genetic manipulation, there exists the risk of attempting to mess with the growing capabilities of some animals such as cows or chickens in an attempt to have them yield larger quantities of meat. Though this seems like a valiant and worthy use of science to be able to feed the world, keep in mind that you're reading this book because you're now dealing with some type of giant monster. This means that every noble attempt has gone horribly awry, and you're now faced with some kind of giant cow that is stampeding across your front lawn.

The other field of concern comes in the form of advanced technology. The technologies in particular we will look at are machines designed to aid in the genetic manipulation of living beings. One of the most common concepts presented in media and literature is the idea of rays that enlarge creatures from their original size and allow them to grow into something that becomes dangerous. Though the device is no doubt created in the same vein of the previously mentioned giant cows, the problem is that the experiment has now gotten out of control and is yours to deal with. Luckily, this scenario won't be hard, as the creature will be close to the facility that enlarged it.

Warnings: Since what you are dealing with has undergone some type of manipulation through science, never automatically assume that you understand what you're dealing with. Now that the creature has undergone the process, it may display characteristics that are unheard of. This means that you will not want to let your guard down just because you are now face-to-face with a 30-foot guinea pig. In fact, until the creature is destroyed or contained, do not let your guard down at all no matter what type of creature you are dealing with.

RFE: There is not one particular course of action when escaping from creatures that were manipulated by science. It is more of a case-by-case scenario where you will have to judge for yourself what type of escape plan is the best. For example, say that the genetically enhanced creature in question is a shark; not a shark that has been altered to be able to walk on the land, but just increased in size. Will you have to worry about it if you live in the Rocky Mountains? Of course not; there is no possible way that the shark would be able to reach you. Instead, stick to the basics and study them in order to prepare yourself for all possible creatures that can be affected or experimented on.

Avoid: If possible, attempt to stay away from the research facility entirely. If you know for a fact that a scientific research base has been conducting weird and unusual experiments at the same time you keep hearing words about people going missing from the area, then there is a pretty good chance that something has gone wrong. Just stay away from the area and you should be all right. People often find themselves becoming the victims of GMEs when they stumble into the classic scenario of "being in the wrong place at the wrong time." This can be prevented by doing research ahead of time and ensuring that no weird occurrences have taken place in the area you plan to take a scenic vacation.

Also, try to stay away from the idea of repeating the same experiment that created the giant monster with yourself as the subject. On paper, the idea to increase your size so that you are somehow able to prove a worthy adversary for the creature sounds feasible. The fact is that this is far too dangerous an idea to simply jump into without proper consideration. Though there is a chance that you will be able to reach an incredible size and hopefully take down the creature with your newfound stature, you must consider what will happen after the battle. Just because you were able to enlarge yourself does not mean for one minute that you be able to reverse the effects of the experiment as soon as the fight is over. If the scientists behind the experiments were able to reverse the effects so easily, then they probably would have done so with the creature in the beginning. As always, don't be rash when making choices in any GME.

Counterattack: As with your RFE, the counterattack for the creature created by science will depend on which creature was used as the subject. Still, one of your safest bets is to try and see if the scientists can reverse the process or, thanks to the extended amount of research information they have on the creature, formulate some type of serum that will be able to incapacitate it. From there, you only have to worry about administering the serum to the creature, but be warned, it is always a bad idea to go after it with only one dosage of antidote. There's no telling if your first attempt will be successful, or if you somehow find a way to drop it and make it unusable.

In the matter of creatures that were enlarged by the means of some type of growth beam, it may be a simple process of changing the polarity so that the device is now a shrinking ray. This will do to blast the creature until it is back to its original size. Make sure that whoever is firing the shrink ray knows how to use it properly, as the last thing you want to happen is for it to break and leave you "up the creek without a paddle." But as mentioned earlier, this solution is not so easily available, so don't bank on it as your only option for dealing with the creature.

DINOSAURS

About: The original giant monsters that walked the earth were the dinosaurs. Larger than life and roaming the earth unchallenged by their sheer physical prowess, these creatures ruled the planet for far longer than any known human civilization. Had it not been for the arrival of a giant meteor that caused the Ice Age, would these creatures still be among us today? This scenario of dinosaurs finding a way to exist in the world we know now has been glorified extensively in different pieces of fiction. Whether it is through genetic cloning or lost eggs that find a way to not only survive the harsh conditions of the earth but also decide to hatch under current ecological conditions, the idea is that the dinosaurs would find some way to become a nuisance for people today. As it would take too long to go through every known dinosaur attack scenario, this section will instead focus on three of the most popular and well-known dinosaurs who ever lived: Pterodactyl, Apatosaurus, and Tyrannosaurus rex.

Warnings: Please recognize that each of the three possibilities presents a different challenge when either planning your escape route or beginning your counterattack. Take an Apatosaurus, for starters. Although it is an herbivore, and thereby will not present the danger of eating any humans, the main predicament comes from its massive size. Studies have shown that the Apatosaurus had a combined weight of at least four elephants, and the notion of an elephant going on a rampage is scary enough to begin with. Try to picture something much larger with a much smaller brain in the modern world with objects and places all around that can easily startle and confuse the creature. Think of what kind of carnage would be caused by that kind of creature stampeding out of control.

Many would consider the pterodactyl to be the least threatening of the three dinosaurs, thanks primarily to the images given off by many movies that depict the creature as simply being a majestic bird of flight from years long past. The fact that is often glossed over is that the pterodactyl was still a meat-eater. It is very important to remember that you, as a person, are made of meat. If creatures enjoy the taste of meat, especially those that are giant in origin, this will prove to be a hazard to your well-being. Although they would prefer to eat fish or scavenge the remains of something that is already dead, the hard fact is that when the moment is right, this creature will eat you without thinking twice about it. Even more alarming is looking at the natural ability of the pterodactyl, which is flight. Its ability to swoop down and pick up an object that it believes to be food is incredibly detrimental to a human, who can easily become a replacement food supply. Don't let your guard down for a second just because this creature has not always been presented as being scary: it has the means to kill you if you are not careful.

The Tyrannosaurus rex needs no introduction when it comes to the idea of how much destructive force it has at its disposal. Enough movies have showcased just how deadly these creatures can be. With a jaw large enough to kill a man in a single bite and legs that allow it to catch up to almost any prey, the idea of this creature being able to run loose in the modern world is simply horrifying. Even one would be able to cause a considerable death toll before it could be stopped. One of the most important facts to keep in mind when dealing with a Tyrannosaurus is that its eyesight is based on movement. This means that as long as you stay still, you will be able to avoid detection. Unfortunately, given the horrific fear that comes from seeing the creature face-to-face, you are going to find it very hard to avoid shaking.

A brief point to make is that, considering the most common place that any lost eggs will be discovered is buried deep in the earth, they are still at danger of contamination from the outside world. One of the most immediate courses of action to deal with the excess of nuclear waste we are creating as a society is burying it deep underground. It is possible that these unhatched eggs may become exposed to this material. Exposing dinosaurs to radioactive material that has the possibility of it mutating them into something unimaginable is extremely dangerous and could result in the creation of a being of unmentionable destructive power.

RFE: Again, when facing the Tyrannosaurus rex, you want to take advantage of the fact that its eyesight is based on movement, which will allow you the time you need to go undetected. Make no movements when the creature takes notice about you until something else catches its attention. After that, the most important point to consider is what kind of vehicle you will be using in your escape. Both the pterodactyl and Tyrannosaurus are creatures known for viciously stalking their prey, so the last thing that you want to do is drive a vehicle that makes a sound like some kind of wounded or injured animal. This will only prove to draw unnecessary attention to yourself and could very well lead to your death. Instead, try to find a quieter vehicle that can still be sure to get you out of danger swiftly and undetected.

Sound is also a factor when considering a vehicle to escape the Apatosaurus but for an entirely different reason. As stated, the

Apatosaurus can be a very gentle creature and only its size poses any real threat. The idea here will be to try and make sure not to startle it in any way so as not to cause it to go out of control. A vehicle that runs silently is ideal here, as speed will not be an issue, considering you will not have to worry about it chasing after you with murderous intent.

Avoid: The biggest temptation when dealing with dinosaurs comes when they are finally captured. Many people want to put them on display somewhere for others to see. Although the idea of a dinosaur amusement park does sound relatively intriguing, the fact is that these creatures were not meant to be showcased— especially if the worst-case scenario comes into play and your newly captured attractions attempt to eat your ticket holders. If containment is absolutely necessary, it is a better idea to consider obtaining some type of remote, isolated area that will allow the creature to flourish without it becoming a danger to itself or others. Especially to others.

Another great error comes in the form of attempting to initiate some type of plan involving the manipulation of weather. Yes, a rapid change in the climate did succeed in halting the activities of every dinosaur and eventually led to their extinction, but it is too risky to attempt today. Weather manipulation techniques are not at a level that they can properly be used as a weapon and could result in a massive change to the environment that could end up doing more harm than the creature itself. Even though the idea of finding a way to create and unleash a blizzard cold enough to stop the creatures in their tracks would be only possible at an extreme worst-case scenario, there are many more options to try so do your best not to jump to the most extreme right off the bat.

Counterattack: Gathering a group of highly trained experts in the field of dinosaur studies to assist in the counterattack should not be a problem at all. Humans have spent decades studying the remains of dinosaurs to try understanding them better. We even created the science of paleontology around such studies. The amount of volunteers to aid you in the takedown and capture will be of no short supply. These highly educated paleontologists will be able to help in mixing the right amount of tranquilizers that will be necessary to ensure a safe capture of the rampaging dinosaur. At the same time, if lethal tactics are necessary, they will be able to offer advice but will probably not wish to, as the idea of destroying a live dinosaur will be off-putting too many in the field.

At the same time remember, as previously mentioned with the

Apatosaurus, that these creatures have large bodies but tiny minds. This means that they are large and lumbering, but they are not cunning in any definition of the word. This will help you sort out a plan to be able to deal with them without any major complication on their part. You might even be able to just use the old carrot on a string trick; only substitute the carrot for a net full of vegetables and the string for an Apache helicopter.

ANCIENT BEINGS

About: So as not to be confused with the dinosaurs, this section focuses more on the idea of sleeping creatures that were sentenced by a mystical force to remain asleep until it was time to awake them from their slumber. If you look back earlier in the book, you'll notice that one of the first things you were informed to do was look for any unusual behavior such as the appearance of a group of people talking about a "great destroyer." This destroyer they are talking about could easily be a sleeping creature that, if awakened, will begin to unleash unspeakable destruction on the world that imprisoned it. These creatures are known for being able to possess mystical abilities that could very well prove to be very deadly and unexpected.

Warnings: One of the easiest ways to deal with this menace is to not let it wake up in the first place. If you are able to stop the ritual from occurring, then the creature will remain asleep and you won't have to deal with the monster going on a rampage. You will still have to deal with an annoyed cult, but worry about that after you take care of the ritual. Disrupting rituals is a very simple process if you think about it in another light. A ritual is basically a recipe, one that if performed correctly will allow the caster (chief/cult leader) of the ritual the means to awaken a sleeping creature. All you will have to do is disturb the recipe and you'll be home free. For example, if the ritual calls for the blood of a dog, replace it with the blood of a cat, and if it demands that the time be exactly on the night of a full moon, simply steal the incantation the cult was reading from and hide out until the moon has changed.

RFE: Resurrected ancient beings are some of the most territorial creatures that you will ever find. The reason that they were put to sleep in their specific location in the first place is because they wouldn't move away and they were disrupting the local population. If you were unsuccessful with being able to stop the ritual and the monster has been resurrected, then for the most part, it will only wish to stay in the immediate area that it originally called home, at least for the time being, until they are fully recovered and can focus on destroying the entire world. This leaves you with the advantage of being able to just leave the creature be without a major risk of being chased extensively. All you have to do is get away from the immediate area and you will be in the clear. Unfortunately, many of you will have a problem with this, as the immediate area will no doubt be your home. Still, you will have to keep in mind the fact that in the occurrence of a GME, the possibility of evacuation from your place of residence is always high, but as long as you stay alive, you will be able to find a way to defeat the creature and reclaim your home.

Avoid: One of the biggest issues you will face will be on a more personal level than anything else. This is because immediately after the resurrection of the creature and the inevitable moment that the creature goes out of control and starts attacking its extremely misguided followers, you will be left with a group of frightened individuals that are directly responsible for the menacing beast that is now about to drive you from your home. It is not uncommon that your first reaction to this will be anger and that the first measure you'll wish to take is to punch the member of the cult that gave you the most trouble in the nose. Instead, try to do your best to contain your anger and realize that these frightened and misguided individuals will now be more than willing to assist you in putting their former "Great Destroyer" to rest. Try to punch only one in the face to let out your anger, then move on.

Counterattack: Due to the fact that the creature will no doubt be mystical in origin, you'll have no choice but to find a way to defeat it in a mystical way. This unfortunately means that you will be unable to receive much help from the armed forces, as the idea of using some 100-year-old talisman/artifact/statue to put the creature into a deep slumber sounds incredibly foolish to someone versed in military strategy. This will leave you with the sole task of finding an individual who will have the ability to use the talisman/artifact/statue that originally served as the source of the creature's slumber and have them perform another spell that will put it back to sleep. Regrettably, there are no ancient sorcerers or witches listed in the phonebook who will be able to help you with your problem, but don't let this discourage you, as you must keep searching if you wish to find a way to stop the creature.

GIANT
INSECTS

About: Many people have a great fear of insects, stemming from the fact that people find them to be creepy, crawly, and just plain disgusting in nature. It is this initial fear of insects that will do nothing to help when a GME takes place involving insects that are now much larger than they ever were previously. The very appearance of these giant insects will cause people to unnecessarily panic, even if the creatures are not in the general area. Panic from others is nothing new to anyone who is preparing themselves for a GME, but few events will prey on people's fears as much as ones that involve enlarged versions of the creatures that they are already afraid of. Keep this in mind as you study the rest of this entry.

Other than the recurring method of science causing the enlargement, insects usually have two ways of achieving their gigantic stature. Both of these methods come from the idea of a lost kingdom. The general idea is that, in a lost corner of the earth, a small area that was once a kingdom or city ruled over by people many years before has been closed off from the outside world. Now isolated, this area becomes infested with insects that without any challenge, predators, or humans to keep them in check have now grown to incredible sizes. There is also the possibility that in this lost kingdom, the insects were already this size and survived without any challenge to their existence from days long since passed. Either way, if there is a rumor of some type of undiscovered lost kingdom that worshipped giant insects, then it would probably be a good idea to stay away from it.

Warnings: The biggest mistake anyone can make when dealing with giant insects comes from the natural reaction that anyone who does not enjoy the sight of bugs will have: basically, an attempt to squish the bug and be done with it. It cannot be stressed heavily enough how this is the wrong idea since these insects are no longer at a level that a rolled-up newspaper can simply handle. Now more than 100 times their original size, the densities of their bodies will be even thicker than that of an adult male. If you actually think you have the ability to take down an adult male in serious armed combat with only a rolled-up newspaper, then by all means go and attack the giant beetle that is charging toward you. On the other hand, if you are not well-versed in the deadly art of newspaper-fu, it would probably be a good idea to not even consider attempting to trample on these insects unless you have a cinderblock on hand that you could easily throw at your enemy. You will need proper equipment if you hope to effectively exterminate these large pests.

RFE: Large insects fall under the category of monsters that tend to remain primarily territorial. For example, if you are facing an army of 10-foot-long ants, you will discover that they will behave and act for the most part like normal ants. This means that they will perform common drone duties including going out and gathering food to return to their colony. This means that your chief course of action will be to get away from the area that the colony has now designated as their kingdom.

Avoid: The biggest temptation to avoid when dealing with giant insects stems primarily from their lost kingdom. If you arrived at this lost kingdom by following ancient legends and texts left behind by a civilization long since dead, you are no doubt here because these texts make mention of some type of lost treasure. Greed has been a downfall of many a good man, and this sin does not disappear simply because you are now in a GME. On the contrary, you'll find that human indecency finds a way to appear at some of the worst possible moments. Overwhelming greed may cause you or someone in your party to attempt to journey so far into the lost kingdom that you are cut off from your escape route and are now surrounded on all sides by the giant insects. If you or someone in your party is overcome by the temptation that is coming from the idea of obtaining an ancient treasure and being able to live like some type of king, then it is time for a wakeup call. No treasure is worth your life, as it would be no fun at all if you aren't around to appreciate and spend it. Keep this in mind if the lure of shiny objects gets the better of you during this troubling ordeal.

Counterattack: Even though you are unable to exercise your original method of dealing with bugs in the form of squishing them, you can still be able to use some of the more advanced techniques that were available to you when they were much smaller and easier to manage. The first of these techniques is the use of pesticides and bug bombs to gas the creatures to death. Understand, though, that the amount of insect poison you will need to kill these bugs is a much stronger and potent dose than you have previously dealt with in the past. Considering that most insect poison is deadly to humans if mishandled in the first place, this new, extra potent batch will definitely be hazardous to humans. Make sure that you are properly protected (it might even be a good idea to consider obtaining some type of hazmat suit with a gas mask to be safe) and that those around you have cleared the area.

A good method which is not as easily obtainable is the use of a flamethrower. Flamethrowers would be a perfect way to eliminate your giant insect problem, except you will not be able to find any flamethrowers simply lying around your local hardware store. Most flamethrowers are only available through specialty locations and services (such as construction companies), and for the most part, require a skilled hand to be able to use effectively. Hopefully, you will have found some division of the armed services who have noticed the appearance of the giant insects and have a flamethrower at their disposal. This will be able to help in the extermination process so that things go so much smoother.

You will also want to avoid using a giant net to try and ensnare any winged creature. It can seem like the most logical step. You have a giant insect: just catch it with a net, put it in an incredibly large jar with oversized holes in the top so it can get proper air, and the problem's solved. What people forget is that an enormous moth with its football-field-sized wings has the ability to generate extreme gale force winds. If you were actually cable of getting some military helicopters and attached the net between them, you'd be sending the pilots to their deaths. The net will create a large amount of drag, and when the killer moth flaps its wings, the helicopters would have trouble stabilizing themselves and end up crashing into one another. Better just to keep helicopters away from any insect whose wings generate any force and just forget about using a giant net at all. Don't always look for the easy way with your counterattack.

GIANT SPIDERS

About: Given the amount of media associated with this particular type of monster, it is a good idea to look at them separately from other enlarged creepy crawlies. Again, the greatest advantage that these creatures have when they mount their attack is that they are the embodiment of many people's nightmares, allowing them to cause panic on a high level. This is especially true given the nature of these creatures. With their ability to spin webs to trap their prey and the fact that their diet consists primarily of eating creatures that they have caught, any unfortunate person who does find themselves trapped will soon be at the mercy of these highly disgusting creatures. You will no doubt have to push through the fear as you fight them or risk getting lost in it and losing the advantage of rational thought.

Warnings: The greatest warning that can be given should be the most obvious one, as long as an individual possesses at least some small level of strategic planning: STAY AWAY FROM THE WEB! Other than their size and their disgusting, panic-inducing physical appearance, these creatures come equipped with one of the greatest built-in traps in the history of the world. The ability to spin a material that keeps any level of prey subdued until they can be dealt with gives them an overwhelming advantage. Anyone who has attempted to remove normal spider webbing from their body has found that it can be incredibly difficult, as it seems to cling to whatever it touches. Think about this clinging material surrounding you like a net. Do you honestly believe that you will be able to escape it as easily as just squirming about? You instead find that your squirming will be your downfall, *as it will cause you to grow more and more entangled in a material.*

If you know the danger that a giant spider's web possesses, you may think that you will be safe as long as you make haste and do all that you can to stay away from the creature's lair. As obvious as this sounds, it is a common misconception. Don't forget that spiders have the natural ability of being extremely well-versed in climbing and jumping. This will sadly eliminate the possibility of escaping to a height that is out of their range, as with their new size, they will be able to reach as long as they have some type of a structure to climb on or jump off. Also, keep in mind that this jumping will make it extremely difficult when attempting to flee, as they will be able to close any gap that you were able to create through excessive speeding.

RFE: One of the simplest ways to defeat any opponent is by eliminating the advantages that it has over you. In this case, you are faced with the difficulty of eliminating the giant spider's advantages of spinning webs, climbing high, and jumping far. Do your best not to be discouraged, as eliminating these advantages are easier than you think. First off, you can eliminate the possibility of getting lost in the webs by getting out of their lair and staying away from any area that they may have had the opportunity to spin new webs in. From there, you will be able to eliminate the second advantage of climbing by choosing an escape destination that is out in the open and causes them to be an overly large target. Finally, you can eliminate the jumping advantage as long as you have chosen a location that allows for only one point of entrance. Perhaps it would be easier if it was described to you more visually.

Anyone who has been to a coastal destination such as Massachusetts knows that there are long stretches of roads that lead to peninsulas that are surrounded on all sides by water. This is perfect, as the area will more than likely have no place high enough for the creature to climb onto and will give you a single point of entrance for you to expect an attack from. The forewarning also eliminates the idea of them spinning a giant web to ensnare you. Some might argue that some spiders do possess the ability to swim and will thereby have another entrance point onto the peninsula, but understand that even though they can swim, they cannot necessarily swim well. An awkward attempt to reach you on the peninsula will hinder themselves, leaving a perfect opportunity to attack them. By choosing this as your destination and spot of inevitable counterattack, you will have limited the playing field enough to be able to take the creature on.

The most reliable vehicle that can be chosen to help you get to a peninsula fastest is a motorcycle. A motorcycle will allow you to get up to speed so you can stay ahead of the pursuing creature. At the same time, it will give you the agility necessary to swerve and dodge if the creature attempts to jump at you while you escape. To be able to evade properly, you'll need to make sure you constantly look back in your mirrors to make sure that the creature hasn't already left the ground and is only a few feet from crashing down on top of you.

Avoid: The most impulsive action someone can take when dealing with giant spiders is to attempt a removal of their webbing through the use of fire. This is an incredibly bad idea as the material is highly flammable and will spread flames to the point that you aren't trapped by the webs, but by a wall of fire. Your newly created inferno will also serve to confuse the creature and send it out of control, which is the last thing you want to happen. To quote a very bad old saying: "Stay away from fire or you will get burned."

Counterattack: The most effective means of getting rid of these creatures will be the use of a weapon that will destroy them all at once before they know to avoid it. See if you can find some type of highly explosive round to fire off, such as a bazooka, which will allow you to destroy the creature in one shot. Make sure that whoever is operating the bazooka is a well-trained professional, because if you miss, you'll end up causing more destruction than the giant spider.

Also, please take care to remember that even after the destruction of the giant spider, your work will not be finished. You will still have to venture into the spider's lair and make sure that you destroy any eggs that were laid by it. Stopping any potential escalating danger associated with the GME can be achieved by taking simple precautionary measures to ensure no more giant creatures are added into the equation. Destroy the nest, and you won't have to deal with more of these creatures appearing in the future.

GIANT
SNAKES

About: Completing the trilogy of creatures that prey on people's fears, we now come to a category that is already a part of the world we live in, but also has a reputation for being one of the deadliest killers in the world. Snakes have always received a mixture of fear and fascination. In ancient times, specific civilizations even worshipped snakes like they were gods. Whether you feel that snakes are a subject of terror or attraction, it is undeniable that once they are large enough to become a threat to man, then they must either be avoided or dealt with accordingly.

Warnings: Snakes have an abundance of speed that many giant monsters seriously lack, making them near impossible to escape on foot. Make no mistake: you will not be able to outrun a snake—even one that is now the size of a house—as it will be able to launch forward and attack before you know what has happened.

Another deadly feature that the snake possesses is the ability to wrap themselves around their prey and slowly crush the life out of them. This does depend on how big of a snake you are dealing with, though. If it is rather small in terms of a giant monster (33 feet long or less), then it will go with the instinctual attack of attempting to crush you. If a snake is too big, it will skip over attempting to strangle you and instead eat you up in a single bite.

A great risk comes from the possibility that you'll be dealing with a snake that has undergone some type of mutation. Not only will this cause the creature to enlarge in size, but it will also cause its natural talents to undergo a change as well. Many snakes have the ability to spray venom at their prey to blind them and make the kill that much easier. A snake that has undergone a mutation, though, could have easily had its venom-producing glands change in a way that the venom is much more harmful than before. In some cases, the potency of the venom may even increase to the point that it actually displays the same characteristics as acid. This means that if you find yourself sprayed by the creature's venom, it may cause severe damage to your skin before the creature has even touched you.

One of the most common mistakes people make when dealing with snakes is forgetting how many snakes can travel through the water and swim at excessive speeds. There have been countless instances where people have tried to escape from snakes by fleeing into water only to discover the snake is still hot on their heels. Do not make the same mistake when you are on the run from a snake, especially one that is giant in origin.

RFE: The greatest advantage you will have in your fight against the snake will be their biology. Snakes are cold-blooded, which means that they must stay warm by remaining in areas that maintain a high-temperature climate. Use this fact to your advantage when planning your escape route. Simply head to an area that is colder, and it will act as a natural deterrent to keep the snake from coming after you.

The best choice of vehicle to use when escaping is a plane. Snakes are creatures that are bound to the earth, and other than lunging very high, they will mostly be unable to reach you once you hit the stratosphere. If you're actually fighting against a snake whose height has increased to a level that it is able to bite planes out of the air, then you are facing an opponent that is too large to escape from.

Avoid: You will need to try your best to avoid getting close to this creature at all costs. Your plan of attack must not, under any circumstances, require close contact in an attempt to destroy it. Once you get within its range, it will be able to either get under you and bite you, swallowing you whole, or coil its massive body around you. Unfortunately, once you are enclosed by these creatures, there is nothing that can be recommended to save you.

Counterattack: Just as with your RFE, you'll want to pay close attention to the snake's weakness of colder climates. Once they reach the cold, they will soon stop moving and allow you a very rare opportunity to go in for the kill. If you can somehow find a way to bait the large creature into entering an industrial-sized freezer, such as the kind found in a meat processing plant, you will have found the perfect cage to hold the creature. Once lured inside, you must make absolutely sure that you have sealed off all entrances and exits to the freezer so there is no chance that the snake can escape, and then turn the temperature in the room down to the lowest possible setting. This will ensure that the creature had been properly dealt with.

BURROWERS

About: This category of monster refers to any creature that lives underground and possesses the ability to tunnel through the earth. These monsters pose a very big threat by exploiting one of the biggest blind spots that humans and many other helpless creatures have through appearing from out of the ground. Even if you are able to eventually spot and recognize the warning signs that this type of creature is in the general area, there will still be countless individuals who will fail to recognize the monster's presence and be killed without even being aware of what has happened.

Since the creature has the ability to tunnel so easily through the earth, it is safe to assume that the creature possesses some form of sharp appendage that is used to shift through the soil. When they go on the attack and find something that they consider food, such as human, they will be able to rip it asunder with these razor sharp appendages too. Take note of these appendages if they are starting to attack and do your best to avoid them.

Due primarily to the fact that they are subterranean creatures, burrowers that still use their eyes to see will more than likely have sensitivity to high amounts of light. This means that if they do decide to make it to the surface and launch some kind of attack on the human race, it will take place sometime at night. This will give them a high advantage, as we humans are not always blessed with the ability to see in the dark.

Warnings: The next problem to deal with is that the creature also has the ability to return to their tunnels and attempt to set up for another attack. If they have designated you as their target, they will try again to burst from the ground and kill you. Even if you find some way to recognize where they will appear from, you still run the risk of being unable to get out of the general area due to their enormous size and speed at which they can tunnel.

Being subterranean, these creatures will not necessarily use their eyes to see when they are getting around. Instead, many others will try to rely on an enriched sense of hearing to detect even the lowest level of sound. This makes it extremely difficult to get away from the creatures, as the sound of your footsteps will give away your position to the creature and draw its attention.

RFE: With the drawback that your footsteps will draw the creature closer to you, you'll have to seriously rethink your normal way of retreating from any GME. Unlike the previously mentioned cases where speed was key to guaranteeing your survival, you instead have to rely on stealth. This means that, despite the fact that the creature has the ability to move at extreme speeds and appear out of the ground at a moment's notice, you have no choice but to move quietly and make as little noise as possible. When you finally make it to your vehicle, keep in mind that it will need it to be whisper quiet so as not to alert the creature. Much like an Apatosaurus, you should not create any noise or risk the consequences.

Another important point to keep in mind is the structure you will be escaping to. You will have to avoid going into any small one- or two-level structures, as they will be unable to provide any type of decent protection against a giant burrowing monster, and at best, provide you with a false sense of security. Instead, consider the option of escaping to a larger building such as a skyscraper, as the giant creature will be unable to take it down in one fell swoop.

A skyscraper can also help by providing two very realistic possibilities. The first is that the destruction of the skyscraper will cause people to finally realize that the monster is attacking, if somehow they ignorantly did not realize it yet. This abundant amount of attention will cause somebody to contact the proper authorities so that the right aid can to be brought in to assist in the situation.

The second favorable outcome is the idea that the creature does succeed in breaking enough of the supports holding up the structure that it starts to fully collapse and crushes the creature beneath its rubble. Though this would serve to ensure that the creature was properly disposed, this outcome does result in a very high risk of casualties. It is a good possibility that a large building will not be completely empty or able to be fully evacuated. Still, if you are lucky enough to be in a building where you are the only inhabitant, do your best to get out in time so the structure can fall and crush the creature underneath.

Avoid: This is another creature that will be blessed with the advantage of having a hazardous lair. It is a VERY bad idea to even consider the idea of going into a tunnel that the creature has dug in hopes of finding its resting place. Despite the fact that the strategy of attacking the creature while it is sleeping will allow you a greater advantage, the trip to the resting place will be a hard risk to undertake. Creatures that have the ability to burrow will be able to dig through every conceivable bit of earth in the general area. This means that it will not hesitate for a second to burst out from the tunnel walls and destroy intruders. The creature will have absolutely no sentimentality over the idea of destroying its work as long as it will be able to eradicate the intruders that are trespassing in its territory.

Counterattack: The fact that these creatures are subterranean will also help you with your counterattack, as any exposure to high-wattage light should cause the creature extreme pain. You will be able to turn incredibly bright lights on the creature and force it back to expose an opening for an attack. Remember that this will only catch it off guard for a moment, so be properly prepared for when you are given this narrow opening or you may miss a valuable opportunity. Also, make sure to wear protective eyewear.

If the creature does not wish to come to play, you will have to start in a different way. Since you'll be unable to enter into the tunnel itself, you must find something that you will be able to send down after the creature. Keep in mind, it is highly ill-advised to go down in person; try instead to get some remote control units that will be able to take down explosives that you can then detonate. This will ensure that you are putting absolutely no one at risk, and at the same time ensure that the creature will be dealt with through the most efficient means possible. Just make sure that the area above the creature's lair has been properly evacuated, as the ensuing explosion will no doubt cause a sinkhole to form.

ALTERNATE
REALITY

About: The purpose of this book is to properly outline and prepare you, the reader, for any possible contingency involving a giant monster. Even the most remote and least possible circumstances have been taken into consideration to make sure that you are properly organized. Probably one of the least-possible scenarios to occur is a rip in the fabric of reality taking place, opening a portal to another dimension, and that a creature of enlarged stature will walk out of the rip and want to destroy the area. Although least likely, it is still entirely possible, and you will still want to do everything in your power to prepare yourself if this event does take place.

Warnings: There is no absolute way to prepare for this event, as it is impossible to list all the different possible monsters that could appear. Other realities could easily contain monsters with different abilities and ever-changing genetic structures. The psychologist William James himself coined the phrase "Multiverse" to describe the possibility of there being so many separate universes than our own. There could be creatures that have 300 arms, require cement as a dietary supplement, or have the ability to spawn more of its kind by simply planting seeds in the ground. An entire book series could be written to properly prepare you for a monster attack from this classification of monsters. Instead, just stick with the basics for an alternate reality creature and do your best not to get yourself killed until you have the time to get away and find the proper scientists who can analyze the creature. After the analysis is complete, the structure of the creature will become more understandable and its weaknesses will be that much easier to pinpoint.

RFE: The rip in reality or portal to another dimension (whichever you prefer to call it) will not simply appear out of nowhere in a moment's notice. Instead, there should be a lot of signs that it will occur. A rip will cause a dramatic amount of energy to be released, resulting in a change in the electromagnetic flow of the area. This will cause warning signs that can include anything from high-electrical storms, to drastic changes in climate, to the appearance of a blinding light. Once these signs have been properly documented, they will aid you in pinpointing exactly where the next rip in reality will take place. Recognizing these warning signs will also help you to stay out of that general area so you can find somewhere safe.

Help in detecting this abnormality will be made available through the help of birds. Birds are known to be sensitive to the electromagnetic flow of the earth, and the appearance of a rift which drastically alters the flow will cause every bird in the general area to scatter and even lose their sense of direction. If an area appears to be having a great deal of birds either acting strangely or falling to the ground, dead from the strain of panic, then it would be a good idea to stay away from the area. This idea should be enforced even if a rip does not occur, for the sake of your own health.

Avoid: If by chance the rip in the realities is remaining open and stable, you should not, under any circumstances try to enter it. Sure, you might be overwhelmed by curiosity or the idea of being able to see what an alternate reality looks like, but understand that it is alternative and could possess environmental factors that our human bodies are not able to deal with.

Let's simplify this incident, shall we? One example is that the air we breathe is made up of 78% nitrogen and 20.95% oxygen. A shift in the ratio of oxygen will cause the area to be much more flammable due to the amount of oxygen molecules that now exists. While at the same time, a shift in the amount of nitrogen molecules will cause the area to become unable to support human beings, as we will not be able to take that amount of nitrogen into our lungs properly. Remember that the rules for alternate realities should never be applied to our own. This means that you're unable to take comfort in the simplest of scientific facts that we take for granted on an everyday basis, such as the previously mentioned air mixture. The air mixture of the alternate reality could very well have an increase in the amount of carbon we find in our own (only about 1%) which could cause any individual that wandered into the area to suffocate almost instantaneously.

Additionally, you're not even sure what will happen when you enter into the alternate reality. You have no guarantee that you will step in one way and come out the other side safely. There could very well be too much energy in the portal, causing you to be ripped apart once you step inside. Many of the giant monsters that we have covered in this book previously have been known to have body structures that endure large amounts of punishment and act as a defensive tool. These body structures could very well be what allowed the creature to pass through the portal unharmed, but you as a human being may not be so lucky, as our bodies are fragile and have a tendency to break far too easily.

Only through proper study will it become even feasible to be able to face the creature or enter into the alternate reality. Once the appropriate amount of information is gathered and specialty equipment has been obtained, you'll be able to venture into the reality so you might see firsthand what kind of environment was able to produce a massive creature.

Counterattack: Make sure that you are not too quick in starting your counterattack. As stated earlier, you have absolutely no information on this creature's anatomy. As such, you will have no idea what will happen if and when the creature is destroyed. For all you know, it could very well release a deadly toxin or infectious bacteria that could destroy all life on the planet. You will not want to make the situation more problematic than it already is. Wait for the research to be done first so you are able to attack without having to worry about the possibility of inadvertently destroying the entire human race because you killed the rampaging monster.

Scientists will prove to be of the greatest aid in assisting in this situation. Once they are able to conduct and study both the creature and the rip in reality, they will be able to properly advise on the recommended course of action. The best outcome is that they will find a way to close the rip and make sure that no other portals appear. If they do find a way to close the portal, you will need to find a way of luring the creature back into the dimensional rip and closing it so there is no chance that it can come back through. Again, exercise extreme caution because there is no way of telling what will happen if you get too close to the portal.

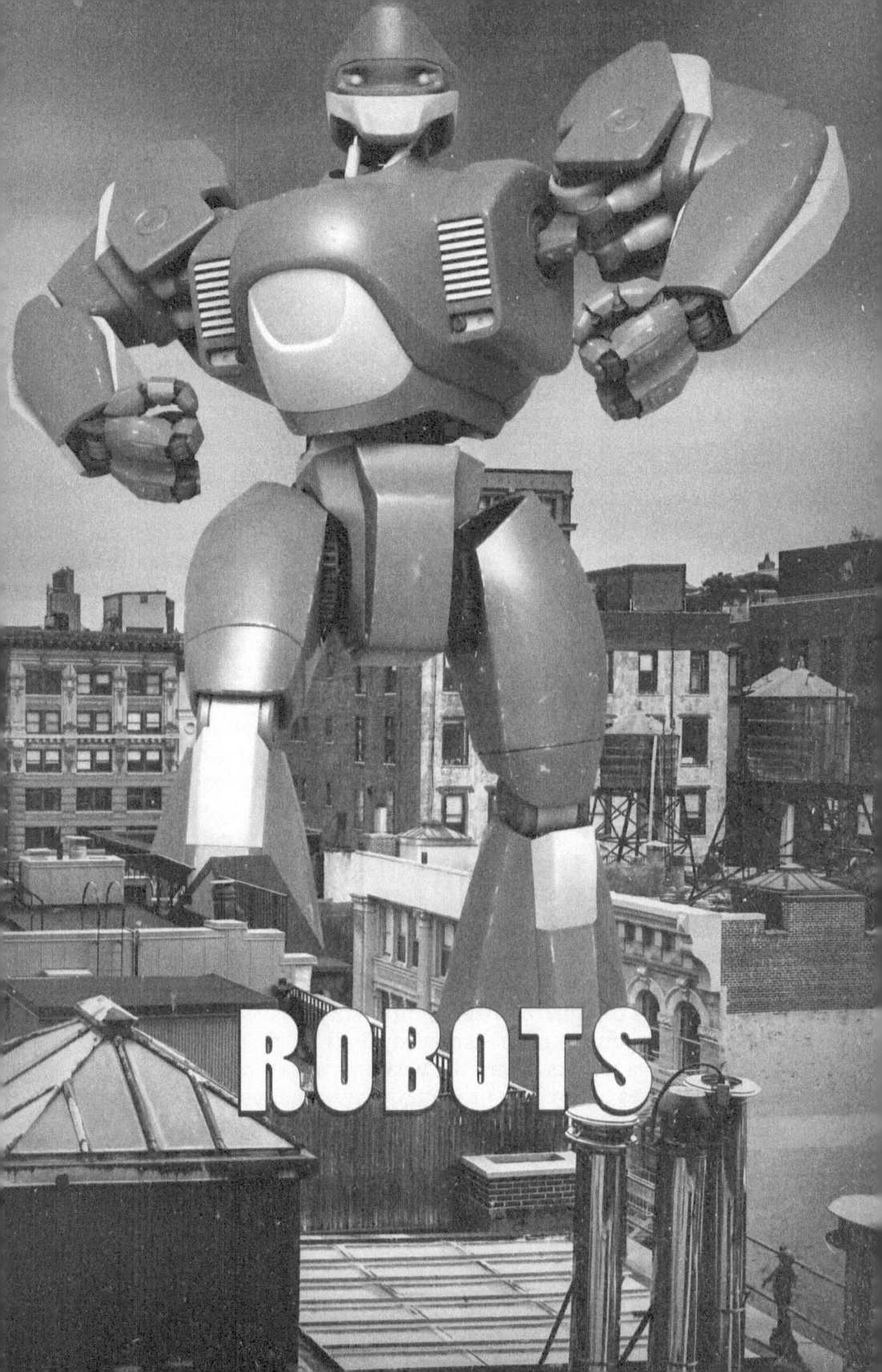

ROBOTS

About: The idea of a giant robot has always been talked about, but back in the day, it was simply dismissed as being impossible to achieve. As science progressed, though, and technology advanced by leaps and bounds, the concept of a giant robot no longer seems far off in the slightest. Even if you ignore the possibilities of a giant robot coming from space or an alternate reality, the idea of creating one with modern day technology and an infinite amount of resources does not seem infeasible at all.

Advances in the field of metal manipulation have resulted in being able to create structures that were previously unthinkable. These structures are able to withstand much more punishment than previously conceived. This means that if there was an experimental robot being developed and it was to go out of control, it would no doubt be made of a material that is both bulletproof and weather resistant. This eliminates the possibility that normal arms fire will be able to penetrate its hull or that extreme weather conditions will render it inert. Robots from space and those from alternate realities will have just as much if not more of a protective hide than the ones we would have through our technological limits. Space robots will have the ability to not only fly extreme distances but also enter into the Earth's atmosphere without any difficulty. Robots from alternate realities will have the ability to walk through a dimensional portal without any complications because their structures can withstand the extreme energies that are released in the portal. Keep this in mind before attempting something as foolish in your counterattack as running at it with a lead pipe, fire axe, or any other hand-held weapon that you have at your disposal. You're going to be dealing with something far more complex than just brute force and must try to find more advanced materials for dealing with this threat.

Warnings: Do your best not to underestimate this creature at any time. Robots are usually known to be built with advanced weapons systems for the purposes of defense or, depending on the original concept on its design, offense. Additionally, they will not always have the weapons readily displayed; instead, they may possess hidden compartments where the weapons are stored when not in use. This serves to not only protect the weapons systems from any attack, but also catch an enemy off guard when they misjudge the extent of the robot's abilities. Don't forget that the weapons that they are storing are made intentionally for killing, and you stand little chance once they are finally deployed. This idea is backed by the fact that most giant robots are created through military contracts and are thereby meant to be used for combat purposes.

Unless the robot's programming has totally gone haywire, sending it on a berserk rampage to destroy every living thing in sight, it will simply operate under the guidelines of self-preservation and defense. This means that unless you attack it head on, it will ignore you in the long run and simply move on. Don't be a hero if you don't have to. It is always recommended that you take the safest available method of getting out of the GME in one piece. Though if it has been given orders to attack you by some type of mad scientist or deranged dictator, that is another story entirely. In that case, you definitely should run like crazy.

RFE: Escaping from an attacking giant robot will be one of the hardest conceivable scenarios you will face. Unlike the previously mentioned burrowing creature that possessed sensitivity toward light and giving you an advantage during the day, robots will have few limitations when on the hunt. Because they are robots and possess advanced technology, they'll be able to track you in ways that previous creatures are not capable of: including radar, sonar, night vision, and thermal scanning. Depending on how good these sensory technologies are, there is a possibility that you will never be able to get away from the robot as it will no doubt be able to track you farther than you can run.

The ability to escape to different terrains will be lost as you contend with giant robots. No matter what the terrain, they are easily adaptable and able to find a way around or through it. Forests will not be able to hold them back as they will either deploy blades to cut down trees or simply ignite the forest and walk through the blazing inferno, totally unharmed. They'll be able to fly over oceans or be properly insulated in a way that they will be able to enter into the water without any damage to their systems. Mountains will not stop them, as they will be able to deploy spikes to ensure that they can climb easier or have the ability to activate jets and fly over the mountain. These environments will not be able to aid you at all in the long run, so simply focus on the fact that you need to get away and get away fast.

As you escape, move as quickly as you can and make sure that you do not look back. Your only option will be to focus on speed, ensuring that you are able to get away fast enough that the robotic nightmare is unable to catch up. Focus on a vehicle that provides the most speed available to you. Once in your vehicle, you want to drive as fast as possible to ensure that you are actually successful in making your escape, taking only brief stops to resupply and refuel. If a giant robot is truly on your trail, then you have no choice but to keep running and wait for the armed forces to launch a counterattack to give the creature something new to contend with. This will change its priority from tracking you down to defending itself, giving you the time you need to find safety and join the armed forces in making sure that the robot is properly destroyed.

Avoid: The greatest cliché associated with robots is that they are totally unable to function once they get wet. With technological advances being what they are, robots no longer have this overwhelming weakness. As mentioned, most of today's robots will be properly insulated so they do not risk shutting down by simply stepping into a small downpour. This means that turning a hose on a robot will do no good and just waste valuable time you could be using to make your escape.

Counterattack: With the loss of water as the primary element in dealing with a giant robot, you must find a way to destroy the technology on the inside. Your first option is finding a way to replicate an electromagnetic pulse (EMP). An EMP serves to create surges in electrical equipment within the area it is released, rendering affected pieces useless. An EMP used on a giant robot will cause it to shut down and become nothing more than a giant pile of scrap metal.

If you are not fortunate enough to have an EMP as an option (maybe because the robot has EMP protection of some kind), you may find something more readily available: electricity. If you're able to find a way to run a pure electrical current into the robot's body, you will be able to overload its systems and fry them. The downside of this is there is no telling how much electrical current will be necessary to properly disable the robot's systems. Depending on how advanced the technology is, it could take the voltage necessary to power an entire city to defeat the robot. If you do not have enough, your attack will be meaningless, and you will have critically delayed yourself.

With the help of the right people on your side, you will be able to take another route in your counterattack. Keep in mind what you're dealing with is a machine being run by a very complex computer. Hopefully, the team at your disposal will be blessed with someone who has a gifted understanding of computer systems and will be able to formulate a virus that can shut them down. You should be aware that, since this robot was originally intended to be a weapon, the possibility of such an attack has likely been considered, and you will have to deal with antivirus protections put into place to stop this very sort of thing from happening. The virus you will need will have to be of superior quality and may still get deleted before it can do any real damage.

We have assumed so far that what you are dealing with is a robot that is unmanned and controlled by an artificial intelligence program. If you find yourself facing off against a robot that is instead controlled by an onboard or remote guidance system, you will be blessed in a way of being able to take down the robot more effectively. Simply find a way to override this guidance system or capture and subdue those that are controlling it. The downside to this idea is that you will actually have to find a way into the robot which may require you to find the blueprints for the robot. If the person who is piloting it is smart, then they more than likely destroyed the plans to ensure there was no way to find a weakness or a back door to the robot. This will make entering and wrestling the controls away much more difficult.

DRAGONS

About: One of the greatest mystical creatures throughout all of history, dragons have been revered for centuries as creatures of legend possessing grace and power. Dragons have been celebrated in different forms of media throughout the world. Sometimes they have even been re-imagined as creatures of great knowledge and wisdom, possessing strength and patience that many humans lack. Even to this day, people look at dragons as a source of wonder and joy when creating works of fiction and art.

Despite the fact that dragons have been worshiped to this day, the purpose of this guide is to prepare you, the reader, for a possible attack from a giant monster. Like it or not, the dragon is a form of giant monster, and in this case, will be viewed as a creature possessing a great deal of destructive power but little intelligence. The idea of a dragon being a creature of great carnage is nothing new, as tales date back long-ago of times when knights would ride off to face down mighty dragons to protect their kingdoms. Unfortunately, many of these knights would end up destroyed by the very creatures they tried to kill. This can be viewed as a testament to underestimating the power that the dragon holds.

If a dragon were to be released on the world, there would be some skeptics who would wish to see it be preserved, but keep in mind that these are truly barbaric creatures. You may even find yourself having to deal with saboteurs who would prefer these creatures repopulate. It is almost romantic to think about one or two dragons defying the odds, evolution, and the world around them to try and re-create their species. Consider the scenario that instead one or two eggs at a time, dragons were similar to salmon and laid a bunch of eggs all at once. This would result in a massive breeding cycle to the point that the dragons could find a way to repopulate the earth and overtake us humans. Stop this overpopulation before it even has a chance to occur and destroy the dragons and their eggs at once.

Dragons are a classification of monster which prefers to behave in a more territorial manner. A dragon, for the most part, will find one particular area to call its own, create a nest, and will prefer to sleep in its newly formed lair more than anything else. Though it might be tempting to see what a dragon's lair looks like, understand that since they are territorial creatures and will look upon you as simply a minor annoyance, they will rip you apart to make sure that you are no longer that annoyance. As always with territorial monsters, if you have the option of staying away from their general area, make absolutely sure that you do.

Warnings: The three biggest problems you face when fighting a dragon come when looking at its three greatest abilities: its armor, its fire, and its ability to fly. A creature possessing any one of these abilities would make for a difficult GME, but to face them all combined makes it extremely challenging. You'll need to be able to make plans and preparations to extremely cautious attacking in these creatures. Let's look at them one at a time, and see if we can't formulate a plan from each.

The first of these to deal with will be its armor. Dragons are known to be thick-skinned to the point that their hides can easily deflect and break metal weapons. Despite our technology, the first things we will go for in an attack are our swords or as they are better known today, our guns. Just like the broadswords of the past, normal ammunition will be unable to pierce the hide of the dragon. Instead, the bullets will simply bounce off and possibly annoy the creature to the point that it decides to attack you fully. Only ammunition made to pierce thick-skinned animals such as elephants or rhinoceroses could stand a chance of being able to do any real damage to a dragon. Remember, if you do not possess any specialized ammunition, you could be spelling your own doom by attempting to take on these creatures. Don't fight them until you're properly armed.

This armored monster will be aided by the fact that it has great agility and flight. Dragons have been drawn countless times over the years possessing large, bat-like wings on their back. With these wings, they will be able to cover much more ground than some of the other giant monsters that lumber due to their enormous mass. Though proper documented evidence has yet to be obtained, it is safe to assume that a dragon will be able to travel at a speed of at least 50 mph. Keep in mind when you plan your escape that you'll need to keep a constant speed of more than this if you hope to make it away safely.

Finally, the most dangerous ability that dragons have at their disposal is fire breathing. Though proper documentation from ancient times has never clearly survived (more than likely due to fire damage), it has been said that dragonfire can be hot enough to melt the weapons and armor of the knights that would attempt to vanquish it. Considering that most armor and weapons back in the day were made of cast iron, and taking into account the melting point of this material (1370 °C /2500 °F), it is safe to assume that the dragon has the ability to summon flames exceeding these temperatures in a matter of moments. Since the action of breathing fire usually had a way of catching knights off guard, it is safe to assume that there was very little buildup necessary to have the flames reach this temperature. This means a fire attack from a dragon may be possible at any time.

RFE: Avoiding thinking about getting into a plane if the GME taking place involves dragons. Dragons are fierce creatures, and for the most part, will look upon any person, animal, or vehicle that enters into its territory as hostile, immediately going on the attack. Planes and helicopters of any size are loud enough to get the dragon's attention. Smaller planes such as ones that fit two people will be crushed in the dragon's mouth with a single bite. A larger plane will simply become a buffet for the creature to enjoy to its heart's content as it peels away the top, sticks its head in, and eats the passengers one at a time. There's no telling how high the dragon will be able to fly, so the possibility of escaping by plane to a higher altitude will not be available, either.

Consider instead, the option of finding a small and whisper-quiet car that is painted in very dark and non-eye-catching color. This small and quiet vehicle will allow you to move away from the dragon's area in a way that does not draw any attention to yourself. Don't worry about speed in this case; only worry about getting away, as you will not wish to appear as an animal that a dragon may want to eat as its dinner. Instead, just slowly drive away, using as many back roads that will allow you to stay somewhat concealed. Do this until you are safely out of the dragon's area.

Avoid: Make sure not to attack the nest of the dragon until you are absolutely sure it has been destroyed. A female dragon is the equivalent of a female lioness: if you mess with her cubs—or in this case, eggs—she'll do everything in her power to make sure you pay for it. Though destruction of the eggs is very important to make sure the dragon population does not increase, you'll want to make sure that you do this only after the mother is dead.

Also, avoid the idea of thinking that these creatures are somehow cold-blooded or should be treated as such. It makes logical sense to think that the best solution for dealing with a creature that can breathe fire is by trapping it someplace cold to keep it out of harm's way, but this is a bad idea. The fact is that the fire will allow it to remain safe even in the coldest areas on the planet.

Counterattack: More than anything else, you'll want to make sure that when you do start a counterattack, you have access to some flame-retardant equipment. If you do not have access to protection, you do nothing but ensure your own demise when the dragon defends itself. Keep this in mind when gathering your materials to ensure you do not bring equipment that will be highly damaged or even explode when brought into contact with fire.

Attempt to find weapons that will be able to give you the distance you need, such as remote control drones or even guided missiles. There are many missile systems that don't even require a jet to fire and will allow you to launch and fly much faster than the dragon will be able to get away. Since dragons are fast in the air, we humans will have to use devices that can move much faster.

SEA
CREATURES

About: The fear of creatures of the deep has existed in the world of man since we built the first boat and sailed across the water, unaware of what could be lurking underneath. To this day, creatures of a large mass and extreme size still exist in the oceans all over the world, some that even make humans appear as mere insects next to their colossal stature (a later section of this book will look at some of the different large ocean creatures that still exist in the world).

There are many enormous creatures in the oceans that never conceive of harming humans in any way, shape, or form. Still, for now, we will exercise the possibility that a large creature from the sea has gone on the attack, obtained a taste for human blood, and thereby must be dealt with effectively. The type of sea creature we will be looking at is the kind that is mandated to stay in the ocean and, unlike the atomic creature, has not mutated in a way that will allow it to venture onto dry land and exact retribution for the nightmarish mess it has now become.

Warnings: Don't go near the water unless you absolutely have to. As always, if you know the situation has the possibility of escalating to a GME, then it is best to stay away from the general area rather than risk your health and well-being by sticking around. If there have already been several reports of ships being sunk or people mysteriously gone missing while swimming, then there is a good possibility that a giant sea monster is on the loose. Unless for some reason you are absolutely mandated to go near the water, such as seeking revenge against the creature for taking a limb and only by killing it will you be able to feel properly vindicated, then your safest bet will be to just stay out of the water and on dry land where the creature will not be able to go.

RFE: If for some reason you find yourself having to head out to sea (such as REVENGE), then by all means make sure that you are using the correct craft. In this case, you want to use a fast enough boat to allow you the option of getting away if the creature does catch on to you. Once you do find a way to accelerate to the point that the creatures can no longer follow you, make sure to head back onto dry land and stay there.

Though it might be more tempting to take a more medium-sized boat, such as a fishing boat, that could hold more equipment to deal with the situation, it would be a disastrous choice in the long run. The larger the ship, the larger the target the creature will be able to attack, and you no longer have advantages in speed and agility to evade it. Unless, of course, you have a battleship. Once you reach the size of a battleship, you will be able to carry not only enough equipment to study the creature, but have the option of unleashing your weapons and destroy the creature if worse comes to worse. To recap, either shoot for extremely large or extremely small when selecting the proper vehicle to take out to the water.

Avoid: A potentially large obstacle you may face when dealing with a large sea monster is the appearance of protesters. Protesters have appeared over the years due to there being many countries that have not treated the oceans with the respect they deserve. Once word gets out that a creature of large magnitude has been sighted in the ocean, there are many who will wish that the creature go unharmed. They will insist that the ocean has plenty of room to facilitate the creature and allow it the possibility of roaming freely. While they may raise some good points, protesters will unfortunately fail to see that the creature is not something that is as gentle as a whale, but it will instead become so wild and uncontrollable that it is a threat to not only itself, but the ecosystem as a whole. This means that you'll have to ignore their words and focus instead on taking out the creature to ensure that it does not destroy the oceans in the long run.

Counterattack: Remote weaponry will once again be beneficial when looking into how to exterminate the creature. With a mixture of sonar and radar, you'll be able to discover where the creature is and track it until it starts to rest. While it is immobile, this will be your primary opportunity to strike. With the use of depth charges or even waterproof dynamite, you will be able to attack the creature from above while also allowing yourself the necessary distance to avoid injury during the attack. Depending on how much equipment you have access to, you may find yourself able to use long-range torpedoes to blow up the creature. Remember, there is no such thing as overkill when dealing with a giant monster; better to be safe than sorry.

Just to be on the safe side, you may also wish to have harpoons at the ready on your vessel just in case the creature does find a way back to the surface. Harpoons are a good idea if you are attempting to explore an area where a giant monster has been reported, as they can be used defensively to stab at the creature and force it to release your vessel, granting an opening to get away at high speeds.

RIP IN
TIME/SPACE

About: One of the other ways a dinosaur might find a way to appear before humans (other than the whole lost world or cloning methods) is through a breakdown in the time-space continuum. This will allow portals to past moments in time to randomly appear and unleash the havoc of history across the world, potentially allowing creatures from the Jurassic, Mesozoic, and even the Ice Age to run rampant in our day and time. Depending on how many portals appear, you could have the entire first Thanksgiving dinner appear in your backyard and a flock of dodo birds appear in your front. Things will get out of hand at an alarming rate.

Warnings: This is another instance where science is your friend. You will have to consult some experts on space and time who will be able to help you define how these portals are appearing. (A/N: Sadly, the writer of this guide is unable to give you the exact home phone number for Stephen Hawking, but there is a pretty good chance he'll be incredibly busy once this event takes place, anyways). Heading to a rather large university, provided you know they have a laboratory more dedicated to physics, is probably the right way to go. You need to know when these portals will appear out of nowhere or you will never have a moment's piece of mind. Just when you think you can relax, BAM! A portal to the past appears before you, and you're staring down a saber-toothed tiger as big as your car. Not exactly the way you want to be spending your Saturday.

There also is the much more gruesome possibility that you find yourself standing in the exact spot that a portal opens. As an individual who doesn't possess a Doctorate in Quantum Physics, it's impossible to tell what exactly will happen to you. All that can be said is that there is a pretty good chance you won't survive the experience. Find out where, when, and how the portals form and you will be able to avoid any unnecessary messiness.

RFE: Now that you have the science and know where portals will form, you will have to diligently plan how things will move. Think of it as planning a parade; one where you have to navigate through the twists and turns of the city without running into any civilians or buildings. Better yet, the more appropriate analogy here would be to think of it as your maneuvering through a battle zone filled with mines, enemy fire, and napalm. Consulting an individual who has experience studying ancient battles is probably one of the best courses of action. You will need to have the most direct route possible to be able to accomplish the goal of an effective counterattack.

Avoid: The rips in space and time will not only allow creatures from the past that are far more massive in size than we are, but also allow some humans to stumble into our time as well. Although it is always polite and courteous to offer aid to people who are victims in a giant monster attack, you have to make sure you are not getting attached to individuals that are from out of our time. If you fall in love with some Juliet from the middle ages, and you decide she would be the perfect person to take on a date, just keep this in mind: if she doesn't return to her time, she will not be able to fulfill her story in history. She could be someone's mother, grandmother, or great-grandmother, the muse that inspired a great artist to paint a masterpiece, or even a brilliant inventor that had no choice but to disguise herself as a man so others would take her work seriously. Keep this idea at hand and don't go smooching up with her.

Counterattack: If there is one rip in the time space continuum, there could be others. Consider the option of looking around for other anomalies and patterns similar to the one that occurred when the dinosaurs appeared. If you are fortunate enough, there will be a rip in time to the future. In the future, get some sweet future technologies including laser guns and computer-based weaponry. If you're lucky, you might even be able to score yourself your own giant robot. These will help you to effectively rid your current time of any disasters from the past.

A bonus that comes with grabbing some tech from the future, other than possibly being able to defeat the giant monsters with it, is that you could make a hefty profit when you sell the equipment for industries to reverse engineer. Just because you are fighting a giant monster doesn't mean you can't think about how to recoup your losses after everything is over. It probably would be smart to make sure you don't sell off anything too dangerous, however. Don't want to be the reason for the downfall of society now, do we?

Chapter 3:
UNDERSTANDING THE
COUNTERATTACK

The most ideal outcome is that you have currently escaped from the area in which the GME is taking place and have made it to safe ground. Congratulate yourself on being able to make it this far. You deserve another round of applause.

What are you doing clapping? This is no time to be clapping; not when there's work to be done. Now is the time to spend getting ready to counterattack. The monster is not simply going to go away just because you hope really, really hard that it does. It'll be up to you to assist those who have survived the initial attack and now wish to make sure that the creature is stopped and its path of destruction halted. So let's get to work.

One of the first things you need to realize is that no man is an island. You will more than likely not be able to take on any giant monster alone and will instead need all the help you can get if you wish to ensure that the monster is handled properly. This in mind, we will take a look at the different organizations and individuals that will be able to help you in your counterattack. We will also look at the some of the more popular methods of battling against a giant monster and go over their advantage and disadvantages.

DIFFERENT ORGANIZATIONS AND GROUPS

SCIENTISTS

About: No matter what the reason for the appearance of the giant monster, whether it is waking up from a timeless sleep, being the last survivor of a lost kingdom, or experiencing a freak mutation, a scientist from some field will eventually come along with the hopes of studying the creature and gaining the scientific knowledge that the creature holds. Whether they had a hand in the creation of the creature could cause them to be drawn to the scene quicker than if they find out about it through a media outlet. For the most part, though, these will be some of the first individuals you want to get in contact with when you finally have the time to get communications up and start to reach out for people who are willing to help you with your current giant monster problem. The creature might have destructive power, but a good scientist behind you having the know-how might just provide you with you need to survive.

Avoid: One of biggest hurdles you'll have to get over when encountering scientists is making sure you can interact with them properly and avoid complications. A particular complication will be the discovery that this scientist or team of scientists helped to create/resurrect/modify the creature that is now stomping around the city and destroying all in its path. You will probably want to do your best to try and keep your anger in check when you come across this information. Yes, it is very tempting to just let it all out and keep punching them until they are out cold, but keep in mind that they have seen the error of their ways and wish to repent in such a way that they will help you get rid of the giant monster. Instead of knocking them out cold, consider just one quick punch to the jaw with enough force in it to throw them off balance and onto the ground. Now, as a gesture of good faith, extend your hand and help them up so the two of you can get to work in your counterattack. Remember: one punch, then get to work.

Forget the option of allowing the scientist the possibility of preserving the creature for study while it's alive. It can be understandable that they will want to take large portions of the creature's biological material back for study in a properly funded and equipped laboratory, but you'll want to clarify what is most crucial. Help them to understand that while the idea of capturing the creature and finding some large, homemade zoo to keep it in sounds all well and good, it will not be possible. They will need to see that the best course of action is to just get rid of the creature with some type of scientific experiment or device so that they do not risk the scenario of the creature getting out and destroying the city again.

Another bad idea with a scientist studying a creature is that they may wish to attempt to clone the beast. Whether it would be to understand the creature better by cloning and raising it from a young creature into a full-blown monster, or for the purpose of being able to fight the original monster it was cloned from, cloning is a bad idea in the long run. There is no guarantee they will be able to create a creature that is exactly like the original and instead might spawn something that has developed genetic defects in the cloning process. In this case, it more likely will not be the genetic defect of gaining the ability to spit acid but will instead probably be created with less brain functions than its original and a highly shortened lifespan.

Also, even though they have succeeded in cloning the creature, what then? Do they actually have some type of method for controlling it properly? Some means to ensure that it will not go out of control? They can't just clone the creature, throw it out into the world, and hope that it will grow a conscience and decide to destroy its original. For all you know, it could very well have the same destructive characteristics as the original, go on a rampage, and then you'll have two giant monsters to deal with.

Consider: After you succeed in talking them down from cloning, try to motivate them toward creating the super weapon necessary to defeat the monster. Help them understand that even though they may have had some part in its creation, and because of it caused a considerable amount of property destruction, that they have a responsibility to fix their mistake. You can be their properly trained assistant who can get all the equipment and materials necessary to ensure completion of the weapon in a timely fashion without any conceivable delays. As always, time is not on your side in these GMEs, so do all that you can to get done as efficiently as possible without cutting any corners.

When the super weapon is finally created and you're about to destroy the giant monster, don't hog all the glory. The scientists who created it would really enjoy the idea of pulling the trigger and making sure that their work was not in vain. Too many times have scientists not had the opportunity to test out their work properly and must watch others use their invention to save the day and take all the credit. Be nice to your scientists, as without them you would not have been able to take down the giant monster that was rampaging through the city.

COSMIC
BEINGS

About: Not all the creatures that come from space will be three-headed harbingers of death that spit lightning from their mouths. Some might actually possess a mind, one that wishes to ensure that the human race is not destroyed by other alien visitors or giant fiends. These noble cosmic beings will journey from systems beyond our own with the intention of doing everything in their power to protect humanity from anything that threatens it. Luckily, they are blessed with not only strength and abilities that humans lack, but also knowledge and wisdom that can help mankind. They cannot just help on the battlefields, fighting with giant monsters, but also help us evolve as a people. One can only hope that we were blessed enough to be able to receive both the aid and pity of these highly powered individuals.

What they hope to accomplish will be no easy task, though, as there are a plethora of incidents that can and will arise that might hinder their mission. To this end, a common occurrence in these situations is that the cosmic being will form a kinship with a member of the human race to help understand our people better. At the same time, they will gain some type of emotional attachment so that when the need comes to fight against an enemy that is threatening mankind, the cosmic being will not hesitate for a moment to jump into action. As you know, forming some type of a bond with anyone when starting a relationship is crucial. The same idea can be inserted when thinking about creatures that are from another planet that may find our ways, customs, and cultures to be somewhat bizarre, and at the same time, fascinating.

Despite the enormous amount of power that these cosmic beings are known to display, the fact is that they are still quite vulnerable. When they are not fighting giant monsters, they usually tend to shrink down into a more compact size or may even return to being just pure energy. While shrunken, many of these cosmic beings will even choose to inhabit a human host body to conserve their energy for when the real fight comes. Do not be alarmed, as these hosts will not be harmed by the cosmic beings inhabiting their body. In fact, the host body may even have some say in the way that combat occurs and can help to bridge the gap between the cosmic beings and the human race.

Avoid: Do your best not to become one of the people who does not trust the cosmic beings. They will have enough to deal with without having to face the possibility of protests and riots from people who do not agree with their arrival. There will almost unavoidably be a group of people who will not understand that the cosmic beings are here to help. They will instead choose to see this new arrival as being no better than the aliens who arrived wanting to destroy the planet. Fear is a natural reaction when people are confronted with that which they do not understand, and it is only through acceptance that we are able to appreciate one another.

You may also find yourself being tasked with the responsibility of ensuring the cosmic being is kept safe. If you by chance are able to meet with the cosmic being, its host body, and the friends it has made while on this planet, you are entrusted with making sure that you are displaying the proper characteristics of a good ambassador and are doing everything in your power to show the cosmic being that humanity is worth fighting for. This does sound like a very taxing experience, but understand that it is nothing compared to the problems that the cosmic being is facing as it continues to fight against giant monsters while being stranded so far away from its home.

Consider: You may wish to consider the option of joining the beings in their fight on a more active level. How do you do this, you might ask? It's simple: all you need to do is gather a group of highly trained individuals, each gifted in a particular skill that aids him or her in combat, while at the same time acquiring some of the most advanced weapons and vehicles on the planet and finally obtaining a very impressive state-of-the-art base to store it all in. OK, probably not so simple, but let's break it down a bit.

When the Earth is threatened by a constant stream of GMEs and a cosmic being has appeared, a call for more immediate action will go up. In response to this call, nations all over the world will band together and pool funding and resources in the hopes of creating a team that will have the ability to scramble at a moment's notice and combat the giant monster scourge. As soon as this team is up and running, they will eventually need more recruits to spread throughout the world to face GMEs, no matter where they may occur. By enlisting in this special team, you will be able to aid the cosmic being in his quest to ensure that humanity is preserved. Waiting on the sidelines for somebody else to get the work done is probably one of the worst courses of action one can take in any GME. Be active and be safe.

THE ARMED
FORCES

About: Throughout this guide, one of the most common suggestions during the appearance of giant monsters has been to find and call on the aid of the Armed Forces. There is a good reason behind this, as the Armed Forces host some of the finest men and women that any country has to offer. The armed services are set up to protect their borders and citizens, and are gifted with some of the best equipment for any situation. This force will be ready at the drop of a hat to mobilize to whatever the situation is and whatever solution is necessary.

The best part is that these individuals are trained and armed with tools to handle a giant monster, no matter in what environment it chooses to appear. They will be able to face it on land, in the deepest ocean, or high in the sky. Through communication with different branches of the Armed Forces, the hindrance of being unable to tackle the situation because you are limited by your resources will vanish almost immediately.

The only major drawback when Armed Forces are called in for assistance on a GME is the time it takes to deploy them properly. When a GME occurs, many actions will have to take place before the Armed Forces are finally given the opportunity to deploy. First, a giant monster must appear, and then it must begin to cause destruction for it to get any real attention. From there, it will have to be such a force to be reckoned with that local authorities will have no choice but to call their superiors and inform them of the situation. The superiors will then begin discussing their options before finally calling the armed services for assistance. Unfortunately, this does not mean that as soon as the Armed Forces are called, they will immediately head out and start to fight against the giant monster. Instead, they will gather Intel and information on the creature to begin to comprehend the situation better, allowing them to mobilize correctly with the right equipment at their disposal. When they finally have a thought-out and detailed plan, they will then begin to head towards the area where the giant monster is located. This will regrettably mean that they must haul all their supplies and gear necessary to handle the situation to the location so they are able to at last get started. Takes a while, doesn't it?

Avoid: Do not let your ego take over and give you a big head over the situation. Yes, you probably were the first people to say that a giant monster was going to appear. Yes, nobody listened to you and the monster went on a rampage that ended up hurting a lot of people. Yes, you have offered valuable information and Intel about the creature just by recapping its movements and its behaviors. Well done and congratulations. Now what do you want, a cookie? A GME does not affect you alone, and it will not be your responsibility to handle it alone. You have to realize that there will come a time and place where you will have to take a step back and let other people handle the situation. Others will have training and experiences you lack that will allow them to be able to face the event in ways that you did not even think were possible. Stay frosty and things will work out.

On the other hand, realize that if an entire army has started to mobilize with the set goal of destroying the monster, then there will be little you can do to stop them. Perhaps you have discovered that the creature is not as bad as you originally thought (though these instances are quite rare), or that the giant super weapon they are about to use will instead cause the creature to evolve into something far worse than it originally was. You need to understand that attempting to stop them at this time will do you little to no good. We are talking about an entire army of individuals here who are on their way to fight with a giant creature. Doing something like chaining yourself to their vehicles and refusing to move on the grounds that they must reconsider their actions will do nothing. Instead, see if you can find a commanding officer who is willing to hear out what you have to say and try to convince them that they must reconsider their actions. Make sure that you have some kind of proof when you make your appeals or you'll be laughed at in your opinion will go unheard. Have strong evidence on hand to ensure that you do not make a fool of yourself so that you can be successful in stopping the operation.

Consider: Take the time to think about giving the forces some assistance when it looks like they are shorthanded during the maneuver. Though they may be properly equipped, the fact is that many a GME is more than the first group of military personnel to arrive can handle. Eventually, they will be able to call in the necessary amount of soldiers to contain the event more thoroughly, but until then, they will need all the help they can get if they wish to be able to stay on top. This does not necessarily mean that you will have to sign up and join the armed services permanently, and once you try it, you might even find yourself liking it. For the moment, however, try and understand that resources will be stretched thin, people will be exhausted, and there will be many moments when others will want to give up. Keep your head held high, and you will be able to make it through the situation and be able to give some assistance when necessary.

POPULAR WEAPONS FOR THE COUNTERATTACK

Many specific items, weapons, and techniques are usually employed in fiction to properly deal with the appearance of a giant monster. Just because these items come from fiction does not automatically dismiss them as being illogical and impossible. You didn't think it was possible for a ravenous 30-foot hamster to appear on your front lawn, but surprise! It's there now. Take a moment to look at the different armaments that can be used to halt the advance of a giant monster. Though some might not be readily available, there may well be an opportunity for them to come into effect.

Robots

When thinking about robots, you must be careful not to group all of them together in one category. There are two main classes that will be essential when you start your counterattack: Androids and Vehicles. You'll want to do some thoughtful planning so that you can properly decide on which of the two is best to use given the situation. You don't want to send out an android and realize that it would have been better to hop into your giant robot vehicle when going off to fight.

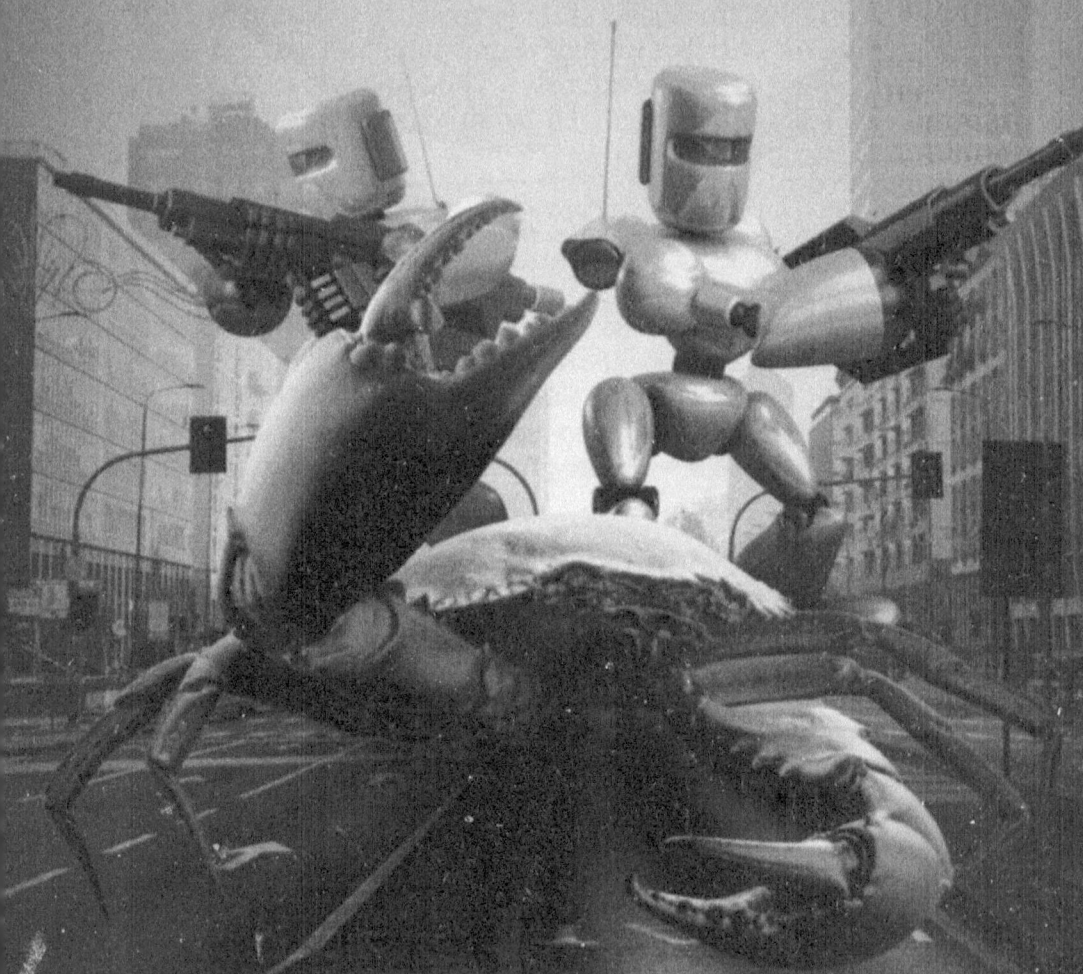

ANDROIDS

About: "Android" here will refer to any robot that is controlled through onboard Artificial Intelligence (A.I.) or remotely through a control device, not just one that appears human-shaped. The size of the androids will vary depending on the model. Some will be just as tall as humans while others will be the same size as the giant monster.

The man-sized android will primarily serve as a type of reconnaissance device that can be sent into a creature's lair to spy on it without running the risk of losing a life in the process. In some extreme cases, you may be able to have the robot go on a suicide mission to ensure that the creature is destroyed properly. Think of how effective it would be if you arm the robot with explosives, infiltrate undetected into the monster's lair, and simply walk into its mouth while it's sleeping, detonating from within. Be warned that if the robot is programmed with self-preservation, it will be hesitant to want to detonate explosives and destroy itself. Make sure you know whether the robot is programmed with this function before you send it on the mission. The last thing you want is for the robot to get all the way there with the explosives and then decide that it will not detonate, leaving you scratching your head and out of luck.

The other option is when the android is the same size as the giant monster that is attacking your town. Usually, through a remote control device, you'll be able to move the robot as you see fit and have it engage in combat with the giant monster. This will allow you the opportunity to have the monster "pick on somebody its own size," which will eliminate the greatest advantage that giant monsters have. As long as you have someone manning the control that is able to keep up with the giant monster, you will be able to defeat it with relatively little difficulty. This is especially true if you are fighting with one that has many different compartments each loaded with destructive weaponry. Once you are able to take on the giant monster with a combination of eliminating its height advantage and attacking it with high-powered weaponry, the monster will trouble you no more.

Understand that a robot (either vehicle or android) will not be without its drawbacks. First, you need to understand that even though it is under your control, you are still unleashing another giant monster into the world. This means that even with the best person behind the controls, they will still cause a large amount of property damage just by having the creature move toward the field of battle. It will be up to you to decide what the better option is: unleashing a giant robot that may bust up the area on its way to do battle or allowing the creature you have absolutely no control over to run free until you have a more cost-effective plan. Keep in mind that all of the ammo you fire at the monster costs money, and it will cost more when it comes time to rearm for another mission. If cost is not an issue, then feel free to run wild.

Another major drawback to deal with is the fact that a robot will require large amounts of upkeep and maintenance to operate to its full potential. If the robot is sent out to fight a monster and is victorious, it will have to undergo hours of maintenance, repairs, and diagnostics to make sure it is back at 100% before its next mission. One of the biggest mistakes people can ever make is attempting to send a robot out when it is at less than optimal efficiency or without properly refilling its ammunition, insisting it will be more than enough. Underestimation like this will result in the robot being destroyed because it is not operating at the usual level to which the controller is accustomed. This will cause a delay in the response time between the robot and its controller; one that the monster will be able to take advantage of to destroy the robot. A robot is a large responsibility, and if you are not up to the task, then you'll find yourself taking on more problems than you can handle.

Avoid: You'll want to stay away from one of the most common mistakes in robot construction: programming the A.I. with some type of emotional aptitude to understand humans and empathize with their suffering. The biggest problem with this idea is that people automatically assume the machine will have the same amount of compassion that any normal person will have. Despite the advancements that have been made in the field of robotics, the fact is we are not yet to a level that allows us to perfectly copy human emotions in a way that a machine is able to recognize and act on properly. If programmed too well, you might actually create a robot with some type of identity crisis who will question if what he is feeling is of his own decision or some type of preprogrammed command. Yes, it is as frustrating as it sounds, so it's best just to leave the emotions out and keep the robot to its basic functions.

In the monsters sections of this book, robots were described as beings from Earth because the possibility still exists that even if they are built by humans, they can run out of control. Whether it's being hacked into or reprogrammed in some way, the possibility of the robot going outside your control is always apparent. Make absolutely sure that you don't let it run amok, as the destructive power behind it is enough to level at least three cities before you are able to reprogram it properly. Consider having some type of absolute kill switch that will allow you the option of cutting off all the machine's functions so it doesn't hurt anyone. Make sure that you distinguish this from the self-destruct button or risk destroying a robot that just needed a good defragging of its memory.

Even though the robot has been created with the idea to be a replacement for human life and prevent anyone from dying, it is still an impressive piece of human technology that has only now been able to be revealed because of a GME. Keep this idea in mind before you decide to push the self-destruct button. Make absolutely sure that there is no possible way to stop the monster unless you blow it up. Think of how foolish you'll feel if you blow up your robot only to realize that you still have to take down the giant mutated gerbil that is now destroying the city. When detonating for an attack, make sure that the ensuing blast will be enough to destroy the creature. If you find yourself pressing the button too early and only blowing off one of the creature's arms, then all you'll have is a monster that is now angry and no means of taking it down. Make it count, as you may only have one chance and one robot considering how much these things cost.

Consider: You'll want to consider the idea of actually reading the instruction manual before turning on or controlling the giant robot. The instruction manual will tell you everything you need to know about the abilities of the robot that you are piloting. You don't want to find yourself struggling to take down a giant monster when the whole time your robot was equipped with a mega death ray that could have destroyed the monster a long time ago. Hidden weapons are commonplace on most giant monsters and yours will probably not be an exception. Ignorance such as this is the last thing you want to hinder your ability to destroy a giant monster properly. It might be a good idea to set up some type of simulator and log a lot of hours in it to ensure that you can operate the robot and unleash its peak performance.

ROBOTIC VEHICLES

About: Giant robots that have an onboard operating system complete with human pilots instead of the previously mentioned remote control unit is the main focus of this section. By piloting the robot by hand, you will eliminate the possibility of a communications breakdown when doing it remotely. This will allow you the opportunity to fight more accurately and without having to worry about whether the signal is reaching the robot properly. Ever have problems with getting a cell phone signal? Think of the same thing, but instead of a friend of the other line, there is a robot with the fate of humanity in its metal hands. Think of how frustrating it would be to walk into a dead zone then.

Through an advance screening process, you'll be able to find some of the best and brightest that have more than enough skill to pilot the robot effectively without any worry of choking up at the worst possible time. What you will want to look for are individuals who possess a burning heart of justice, which means people who will not back down under any circumstances, who will keep fighting no matter what the situation, and even in the darkest hour will rise to the top victorious only by the sheer fact that they did not say die. If your screening process is not looking for these qualifications, then you'll more than likely just find pilots who will give up and call it quits under pressure, which is the last thing that you want to happen. Don't trade computer error for human error. Your goal is to eliminate all error to ensure that the robot performs to its highest capabilities.

One of the complications that can occur with being a giant robot pilot is no longer having the safety of being away from the action. You'll need nerves of steel as you go out and pilot your giant robot in a valiant attempt to make sure that the monster in question is destroyed. This is why a screening process is necessary, as it allows you the opportunity to filter out those who will not be able to handle being behind the controls from those that were born and bred to fly a giant robot.

A word of advice for those that do make it through the screening process and have the potential to go out in a giant robot: Give some thought to the idea of actually naming your attacks. Nothing will help you stay focused and in the right frame of mind more than screaming "Death Blitz!" when you fire off a barrage of missiles or "Laser Cutter!" when you slice the monster apart with an intense blast of energy. Though it may seem childish, understand that it will help you to not lose your nerve. When destroying a monster, you don't need any annoying self-doubt creeping in. It'll be up to you to keep a level head in these circumstances, as you will

117

have the fate of the world on your shoulders and, if by chance, you do end up failing, you will find yourself dooming humanity to destruction by the ensuing carnage that the giant monster will create. No pressure, right?

Also, remember that collateral damage and high repair/reloading costs are still potential concerns you'll face when piloting a robot. Just keep in mind that every step you take and every time the robot is knocked to the ground, it is causing property damage, as will any missile or weapon that you fire that doesn't hit its target. This will help to keep you on task and prevent any pilot from going all out and losing control.

Avoid: Although the idea of letting a young boy or girl pilot your robot might come up, do your best to reconsider this option immediately. Sure, it makes sense that, because children are so gifted at playing video games, they will have a natural ability to control the robot without any difficulty, but understand what you are actually suggesting. You are hoping that a child who has not hit puberty will be able to make the complex decisions necessary to stay on top of the situation. Remember also that you needed to find someone who possesses a great amount of courage and a deep sense of justice, or you might run the risk of selecting a pilot who will lose his nerve in dire situations and flee from the immediate area. You'll unfortunately risk a greater chance of this taking place due to the fact that although some kids might talk a big game, they are still just kids and will more than likely crack under the pressure. Keep this in mind before you even think about throwing some 10-year-old in the pilot seat.

Make sure to remember to check your fuel. Though your pilot might possess the previously mentioned burning heart of justice that allows him or her to be fueled by sheer willpower and never give up, the same cannot be said for your robot. Make sure to pay close attention when out in the robots, and if it looks like you will not have the necessary fuel needed to attack, then don't. Those risky all-or-nothing battles where an individual puts everything on the line in hopes of making that last desperate attempt to save the day are foolish. Take the time necessary to check your fuel and make sure that you will have enough to commence the operation or you probably shouldn't go out at all.

Consider: Always make sure to have a few backup pilots. Although you screened to make sure that you selected individuals who possess great courage and would not break under pressure, for the most part, there are still those rare occasions in which individuals feel the creature standing before them is too much to handle and will flee. What happens when your only pilot is the one that just ran away in cowardice? Or a better question is: What if your pilot is dead? Unfortunately, this would mean that you are screwed and should probably just walk up to the giant monster and allow him to squish you rather quick and painlessly. To prevent this tragedy from taking place, you'll probably wish to make sure that you screened a few backup pilots to ensure there is someone who can get in the pilot seat of the giant robot and take over if your previous candidate has curled up into a fetal position and has started crying bitterly.

To recap: Have a burning heart of justice, watch your ammo, watch for property damage, and make sure that you have back-up pilots who will be able to save the day if necessary. As long as you're aware of all of the possible incidents that might occur and can deal with them, then you have what it takes to be able to launch your giant robot. If not, go back over the steps and see which you can improve before you launch.

SUPER WEAPONS

The term "super weapon" here refers to any and all devices that will be created in the hopes that they have the potential of destroying the monster in just one shot or use. Many would automatically assume that this is the best route to take when dealing with any giant monster, but understand that this is not always the case. Before launching any counterattack, you'll want to keep all of your options open to ensure that you pick the one that will stop the monster the quickest way possible while causing minimal collateral damages or side effects such as fallout or mutation.

SCIENTIFIC

A scientifically created super weapon has the ability to either destroy or incapacitate the monster with the press of a button. This usually comes in the form of a ray that has the potential to destroy the monster, freeze him solid, or even affect him internally, causing him to lose control of his bodily functions and pass out. Each of these has its pluses and minuses that must be taken into account before use.

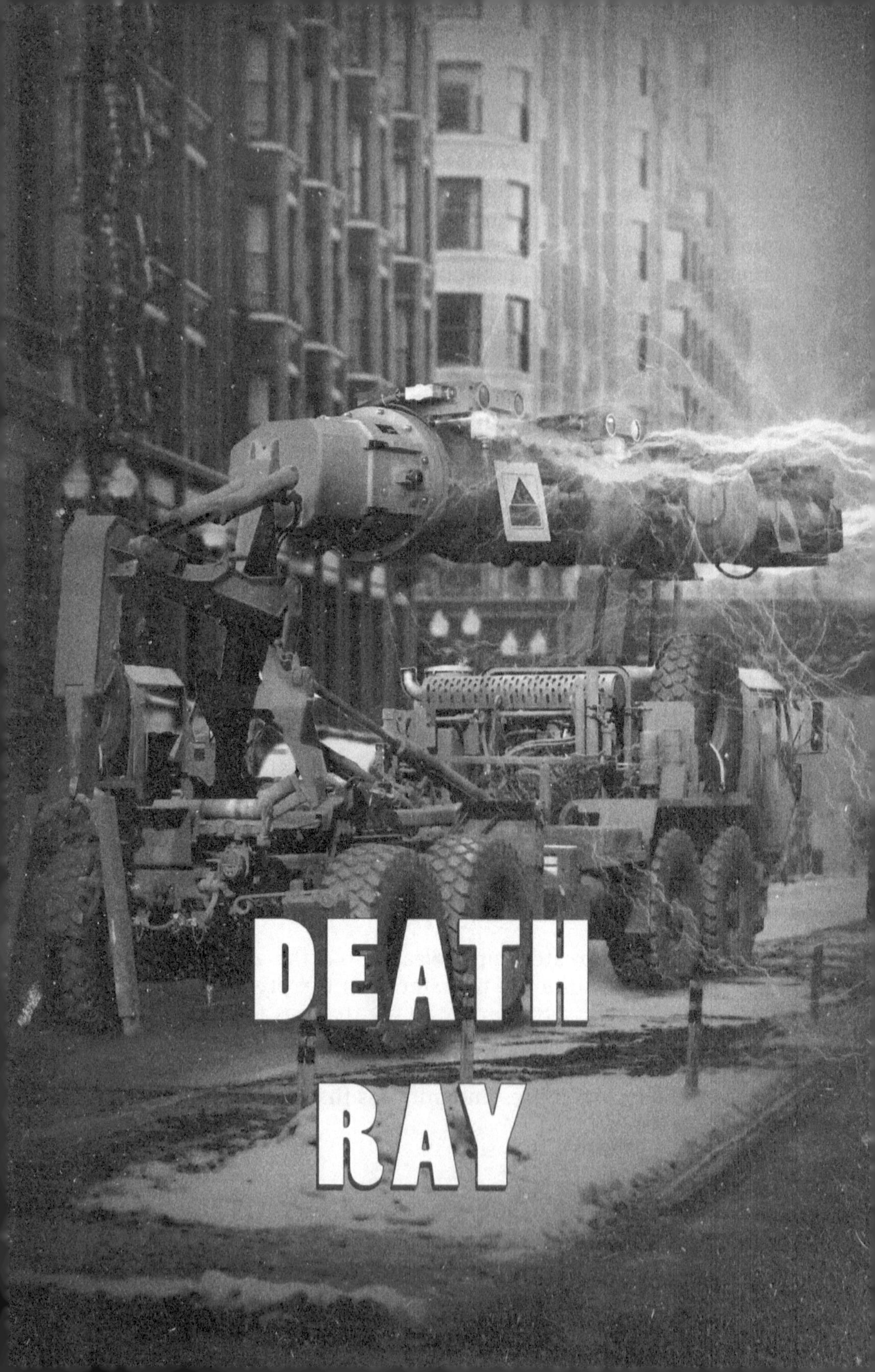
DEATH
RAY

About: The idea behind the death ray is that it possesses enough energy to destroy the creature on a molecular level. This destruction will eventually be enough to slowly wear through the creature to the point that it comes out the other side, leaving a large hole. Usually, a large hole in a monster will be more than enough to ensure that it will no longer be a threat, but if it still wishes to keep going and function despite the fact it has a large hole in its side, simply recharge and shoot again.

Sizes of death rays vary from time to time, but for the most part require the need to be hauled around in the back of a flatbed truck or mounted on a tank. This will limit the mobility of the weapon, as you will have to be in a stock position to be able to use it properly. This is probably for the better, as you will eliminate the risk of missing. Once the vehicle is parked, you have the opportunity to aim at the incoming monster. Make sure that your attack will kill. Don't simply aim for an arm or other appendage; instead, concentrate fire on the main body to increase your chances of hitting somewhere that is able to do some real damage. If possible, you want to destroy the monster's head, which will guarantee a kill, unless of course you are dealing with a giant cockroach (as these creatures are known to survive for several days after having their heads removed).

Avoid: You'll want to be careful on how many times you fire the ray, as it may cause some environmental damage. Too many shots of a high-powered energy weapon will cause the atmosphere of the area to slowly burn up, which could have long-term effects. Think of it as a much more highly accelerated form of global warming but in a particular area and you'll get a general idea of what will happen from excess shots. Make your shots count and you shouldn't have to worry.

Also, make absolutely sure that you don't miss. The ray is designed to deliver an incredible amount of destructive force and affect things on a molecular level. The last thing you want to do is miss and have the ray hit a building or some other structure as it would cause it to fall and be destroyed much faster than if it had been torn down by the attacking creature. Worse yet is the possibility that the laser has so much power behind it that it eradicates most of the West Coast. Nothing is going to be harder than explaining why you ended up deconstructing the molecules of more than half a billion people. Make sure that you aim correctly before you even consider the idea of pulling the trigger.

Consider: With any super weapon, you'll want to make sure you have additional parts to be able to fix it on the chance the weapon was to break down on you at a critical moment. With high-powered lasers such as death rays, you want to make sure that you have some spare lenses around so that you have the option to switch them out in case your first one breaks. The lens controls the amount of power that radiates from the device, which means that a broken lens could cause a loss of control and might even risk the destruction of the device through overload.

A riskier move that might prove to be a safer bet when dealing with a creature that has incredible agility is to turn down the ray and do less damage. A creature that possesses a great deal of enhanced agility, despite the fact it is so large, will make it a harder target to shoot when you go on the counterattack. When you do finally take your shots, a lower setting may provide higher accuracy and more shots, with the tradeoff of potentially taking more time to stun or kill the creature. It may be more time-consuming, but considering what happens when you miss, it might be safer to shoot the lower blasts and not have to worry about whether you'll destroy California.

INTERNAL

DISRUPTOR

DEVICES

About: An internal disruptor causes a creature great discomfort on an internal level, through one way or another. This could mean a highly charged flash that could greatly confuse a creature possessing nocturnal vision or a laser that causes a creature to have bad indigestion. Essentially, the device is made to target a particular function or sense of the creature and overwhelm it to the point that the creature is unable to continue its advance.

Let's try to focus on the use of a sonic broadcast device as sound based weapons are much more commonplace and easy enough to create. You're more than likely to decide to use this device because you are dealing with a creature that has an acute sense of hearing. Just like with many popular dog repellents, you'll want to use a device that emits a high-pitched noise that can only be picked up by the creature and causes the creature to be so overwhelmed that it cannot focus on its advance.

Avoid: This is mainly for the device that causes the creature to have bad indigestion. Sure, the idea seems sound enough that you'd want to throw off the creature by giving it such an upset stomach that it is unable to think properly and becomes confused. In all actuality, you probably want to stay far away from devices that cause the creature to lose grasp of its senses, as it will more than likely begin to thrash around violently as if trying to shake off the confusion that is happening to it. Make sure the device you are working with will instead stun or disable the creature and cease its movements instead of causing it to move around more. In the case of the sonic broadcast device, make sure to find a signal that will cause the creature to want to lie down and cover his ears in an attempt to muzzle the noise instead of one that enrages it.

Consider: Try to find a device that is able to focus on the particular body functions you wish to control. For example, if you think it would be simple enough to just have the creature go to sleep, work from there. It really is not as hard as it sounds; all you need is to find a device that emits electrical charges. Once you have obtained it, you will be able to be launch it into the base of the creature's spine and from there send electrical impulses into the creature's body that will override its nervous system. With the combination of the right charges running through its system, you will be able to take over different motor functions, cause different bodily functions to behave oddly, or (if you are blessed with a truly remarkable model), acquire total control of the monster's movements. Think of how much of a help it would be to have a monster that you could fully control fight against other monsters. (For full details on the aspect of monster vs. monster combat, consult the next chapter of this book).

FREEZE
RAY

About: One of the more peaceful ways of dealing with a monster is to try and capture it. Unfortunately, they are so large that they possess a metabolism that has not been studied by scientists, which makes it difficult to come up with a means of finding a way to subdue them without considerable effort. The idea behind the freeze ray is to project a beam of energy that causes the water molecules in the immediate area to freeze, making ice form on and around its target. All you'll have to do is point the freeze ray at the monster, pull the trigger, and in moments, you will have a giant monster Popsicle. A freeze ray makes the idea of capture more practical, as you have the option of using it to freeze the monster in place and make it vulnerable to transport.

The perfection of the freezing technology has yet to be fully mastered, which deters the idea of using a freeze ray. If you are truly hoping to use one as a way of capturing the creature without doing any permanent damage, you may want to find another method. Most freezing weaponry is intended for use with environmental circumstances, such as to stop rampaging infernos or fires that are unable to be put out by water. More than likely, if you actually end up using the freeze ray on a creature, you may find that it will cause a creature to develop severe levels of frostbite which would mean amputation of limbs.

Avoid: Just like with the death ray, you will want to make sure not to miss with the freeze ray. The device has the possibility to affect both the environment and people around it if shots were to stray off target. The general discharge of the device will cause the immediate area to experience a severe decrease in temperature, resulting in any precipitation in the area to immediately turn to snow, hail, and/or ice. If the environment is not used to these kinds of temperatures and weather conditions, it will result in the deaths of local plant and wildlife that are unable to adapt. There should be no risk of permanent climate change, however, as long as the freeze ray is only shot during one period of time in a general area and not used constantly.

If by chance the ray accidentally hits a person, the results will more than likely be fatal. The device is tuned to be used on a creature that has a large body mass and a much more sophisticated metabolism. This means that if the blasts were to hit a human being, it would result in the individual being frozen solid almost immediately. A more nightmarish scenario is the possibility of the ray going out of control and blasting an entire population that was fleeing from the monster. The last thing you would want to happen is to have an entire group of ice blocks that were once living beings. Make sure that extreme caution when using any of these rays is strictly enforced, as their destructive power should be apparent to anyone who considers handling them.

Consider: If you by chance are an individual who has been studying freezing technology and are on the way to making a breakthrough, you should consider the possibility of selling your patent. As stated previously, freezing technology is by no means a perfect science yet, and any help that can be given to the field is encouraged. Perhaps you have found a way to make a freeze beam cause an ice cage to form around the area that is blasted. This will help by ensuring that it could hold the creature without doing it any injury. Who knows? You might find yourself being the one who is called upon in a GME to use the giant freeze cannon that you are developing in your backyard for just such an occasion.

BIOLOGICAL

Designed more to focus on the body structure of the creature, overall biological super weapons must be handled with extreme caution. Biological weapons designed to work on creatures of extreme height and weight can do incredible damage to creatures of average size. If these weapons were used on a human, death would be instantaneous. Make sure you have all the proper equipment before handling any type of biological agents. In some instances, you might even want to break out the hazmat suit you had on hand for previous events, as it might just help to save your life.

GAS

About: Gas in this instance refers to any type of airborne weapon with the intended purpose of harming the creature. Your overall goal when dealing with gases is to release an amount that is able to overwhelm the creature to the point they eventually pass out.

Certain conditions must be met when dealing with gas to ensure that it does not end up hurting you or your party. First off, you want to make sure to wear gas masks that are able to keep out the negative effects. Second, you want to make sure that weather conditions are just right so that the gas spreads properly without any risk of the wind changing and pushing it in a direction that results in casualties. The sudden appearance of rain would affect your deployment by causing the gas to spread out and thereby not impacting the creature at all. You will also want to watch how you plan to deliver the gas, as the amount required to take down the monster will not simply fit in a gas grenade. The most likely method will instead be a concentrated spray from low-flying planes, similar to the idea of dusting crops.

There are few giant monster types (such as robots or some aliens) that do not require oxygen to sustain themselves in our atmosphere. This means that gas will not be an option as they already have a way of breathing that normal creatures are unable to.

Avoid: Do not even consider for a moment the option of using poison gas when dealing with a giant monster. The amount of gas necessary to have any considerable effect on a monster is already a substantial amount, but when the gas has the potential to kill something that size, the danger level becomes insane. Due to the airborne factor of the gas, there is nearly no way to contain it properly as there is always the risk that the gas will spread into an area you do not have closed off from outside traffic. The worst-case scenario is that the gas turns on you completely and envelops your entire team, which could prove to be disastrous if someone is not wearing a gas mask.

Consider: You may wish to consider all the different possibilities before deciding to use gas as a realistic scenario. Gas has too many factors that can compromise its effectiveness and compromises are the last things you can afford to have when you begin a counterattack. You may want to consider using some type of high-powered tranquilizer or anesthetic instead, as it will be able to affect the creature and thanks to the administrating process it guarantees that the compound is getting into the monster system. You will always have more than one choice when dealing with the creature.

Though it is best to use the idea of any type of gas as a last ditch effort, you may still wish to consider the option of using smoke bombs when you initiate your attack. A properly placed smokescreen will allow you to limit the creature's ability to notice your attack, giving it little time to react and earning you a little bit more of an element of surprise. Make sure to use this sparingly, though, as you are just going to want to put up a covering that allows only a momentary advantage, or you will risk the smoke being too thick and confusing the creature to the point that it begins to thrash about in frustration. Use the proper amount to blindside the creature before it knows what happened.

POISON

About: For centuries, hunters have used poisons to slow animals down, allowing them to finish the poor beasts off without any major difficulty. The same idea will be used when implementing a giant monster attack. The poison will weaken the monster, giving you an opportunity to swoop in for a more effective strike.

Finding the most effective poison will be your highest priority, as you don't want to weaken a monster too little so that you still can't handle it. The necessary amount of poison should be simple enough to find as long as you are properly prepared. Just get a sample of the creature's genetic material and study it for any signs of weakness. Once you have done a proper study, you will be able to easily make a formula that will effectively target the creature so that you are able to ensure its proper annihilation. Finding specialized chemists will help to guarantee that you are making a poison that will have the most effect on the monster.

The easiest way is to administer the toxin is by simply poisoning the creature's food source. Bait a trap with a poisoned amount of food, then lie and wait close by with some type of weapon. As soon as it appears that the poison has started to take effect, you can launch your attack against the creature.

Avoid: Do not try to work with any poison that in some way, shape, or form, alters the creature's DNA. There is no telling what kind of side effects could occur when the administration process begins. You're already dealing with a giant monster, the last thing you want to do is initiate some type of mutation that causes the creature to grow a second head or start to shoot laser beams out of its eyes. Instead, just like when dealing with any type of other animal, simply use the poison that causes its organs to shut down and render it inert. There is no need to get fancy just because you're fighting a much larger creature. You want to use whatever gets the job done in the simplest and least time-consuming manner possible. Just take care of it and forget it: this should be your basic guidelines when dealing with any giant monster.

Consider: Some type of chemical tranquilizer should be the first option if your main goal is to attempt some type of capture-oriented plan. Only through proper sedation will you be able to transport the creature without any major incident. Make sure that if this is your goal, that you inject the creature with enough sedative to ensure that it stays asleep long enough to guarantee proper transport. The last thing you want is for the creature to wake up when he is in the middle of transfer and begin thrashing around inside its transportation container. Just to be on the safe side, you want to consider having guards near the sleeping creature that are armed with some type of device that will allow them to pump more sedative into the creature and keep it asleep. This'll make sure that your creature stays in dreamland long enough for you to get it to its properly designated zone.

VIRUSES

About: Much like poisons, a virus is intended to enter into the body of the creature and cause it to become ill. Also just like poison, a virus will take a while to work its way out of the creature's body, immobilizing it. Unlike poisons, though, viruses are types of organisms that are specifically designed to infect and deteriorate specific cells in the body. This distinguishes them because they are now another form of life that you are bringing into the epic battle, whether you recognize this or not. Make sure that you and your scientists have perfect understanding of the virus before they even consider unleashing it onto the creature and thereby setting it loose onto the world.

Avoid: You'll want to make sure that the virus you plan on using has specific factors that do not target the human body. The biggest concern you'll have to deal with is the possibility that the virus might mutate once inside the creature's body, growing out of control in a form that you are no longer able to deal with properly. Even if it is successful in killing the monster, the fact of the matter is that you will now have an extremely large corpse that is riddled with disease. If you don't have some method of disposing of it, then it probably is not a good idea to consider using a virus in your counterattack at all. Never forget to realize that cleanup is an essential part of any counterattack operation. Don't simply focus on the most immediate problem; try to think ahead to problems that might occur if you go down a particular road. As always, careful planning is the key.

Consider: A step you want to take when using a virus is to have a proper antibody on hand that you can use to stop the virus if it has spread out of control. There is never any way to properly predict how a virus will act or what type of mutation it will undergo, so make absolutely sure that you have some way to halt its movements before it gets out of hand.

UNORTHODOX
METHODS

Seeing as you are dealing with a creature that is irregular in nature, you may find yourself using some fighting methods that are in themselves irregular. Though they at times might feel weird or even silly, understand that they are helping you combat the giant monster that is currently destroying your city. Still, just to be on the safe side, you'll want to make sure that you use these unorthodox methods as last-ditch efforts and only once they have been tested to prove effective against the creature in a way that will be its undoing. If, by chance, the method is not effective at all, it is best to discard it and focus on the more effective counterattack.

SINGING

About: There is an old saying that music can soothe the savage beast. That is exactly what you're attempting when you use this technique in your counterattack. Hopefully, through some odd coincidence or circumstances, you have found an individual who possesses the ability to sing in a manner that causes the giant monster to become at ease or fall asleep entirely. Once you find such an individual, they will become a valuable part of your counterattack.

Understand that this will not be as simple as just having somebody at random sing a few scales and the creature will stop its advance. The particular tone that will stop the monster will no doubt be very unique, and just as there are only a few people who are able to hit the tone necessary to shatter glass with their voice, there will be only a few individuals who are able to sing at a level that soothes the creature. Make sure to play a sample of the person singing over some type of audio device and loudspeaker to see if it has an effect on the creature before making any plans. Also, don't just have the individual start singing immediately after their ability has been discovered, as they will only be one part of a multiple-step operation necessary to capture the creature. Realize that the purpose of singing is to lull the monster into a state of rest and is not intended for destroying the monster on its own. Only through proper planning of the full operation will the singing truly be able to offer any type of value to the counterattack.

Avoid: You'll probably wish to refrain from testing the singing theory when the creature is right on top of you. There is a slim chance that you'll be the exact individual who possesses the necessary vocal pattern to ease the creature, and discovering this at the last possible moment when it appears the creature is about to crush you beneath its heel is even less likely. Even though this is the most prevalent option to avoid, you more than likely will try it out anyway as you'll try anything to make sure that the creature doesn't crush you into a pancake. You will not be frowned upon in attempting to sing at the last possible moment to avoid being crushed, as we can all agree that being crushed is the last thing that anyone would want to have happen to oneself. If, by chance, you are the person who possesses the proper vocal pattern and you were able to stop the creature from crushing you by singing, then congratulations! You not only extended your life, but ensured that you will be a valuable part of the counterattack and may even be noticed by a music executive who will offer you a contract

Consider: To stay out of the immediate danger zone, you'll want to have your voice proceed over some type of speaker system. This is also necessary to make sure that the sound waves are able to reach the creature without having to worry about the singing being heard over other noises, such as people fleeing from the general area. With any luck, the individual will be blessed with being in some type of heavily guarded soundstage that will allow them the opportunity to have their voice recorded. That way, they can enjoy the simple comfort of sipping a nice cup of tea to ensure that their vocal quality does not diminish while being safe and secure. Sadly, not all counterattack strategies will involve a person happily drinking tea while a monster is rampaging through the countryside.

Chapter 4: RAISING A GIANT MONSTER

So you want a little giant monster of your own, huh? One you can find as an egg, hatch, raise and take care of, gently giving baths to, so that hopefully someday it will grow up to be a defender of the Earth that can ward off the advances of other giant monsters? Is this what you are hoping for? The truth is that this idea cannot be immediately dismissed, but venturing into this situation without proper information and an understanding of what you're getting yourself into is highly ill-advised. Take this opportunity to read this chapter and see if you will actually be ready to take care of such a creature if you eventually do find it.

FINDING THE EGG

First, you are going to have to find a giant monster before you even have the opportunity to start raising it. There is no direct way to find a giant monster, being as there's no giant monster pet shop just around the corner. However, as long as you are willing to look in the right area, you should be able to find it.

If you're able to find a lost civilization after falling through a hole in the earth and emerge in a land that time forgot where dinosaurs still roam, tread with caution. For starters, we just said there are dinosaurs around for crying out loud, so do your best not to get eaten. As you start to look around and eventually do find some type of nest, don't immediately walk over and indiscriminately pick up an egg or some newly hatched baby monster. That could very well get you killed if Mama giant monster is around (see next section for more information on that).

Look around until you find a nest that seems unattended and unkempt. You will be especially fortunate if you find an unharmed egg or some wounded baby in a nest that has been attacked recently by a predator and has now been abandoned. It will especially be telling if you find some type of larger creature of the same species dead next to the nest. It is more than likely the parent who has obviously died from either some type of disease or from fending off a predator that was trying to attack the nest (which would explain the other broken eggs or wounded baby creatures you may find). This means that the little creature or egg that you found is an orphan and will have a great deal of difficulty fending for itself in a world as savage as this. By taking it in and raising it as your own, you'll be saving the poor creature's life and help to ensure that it is able to grow up to be a big giant monster, just like nature intended.

Be advised that you want to take a fairly newborn creature and not one that has spent the majority of its childhood in this lost civilization. A creature that has adapted to this lost civilization will no doubt behave much more violently than others and will present extreme difficulty when raising it in the modern day world. If you still feel you are up to the challenge, then by all means, give it a shot. Remember, though, that you were warned of the difficulties you would face so you can't whine about no one informing you beforehand.

SEPARATING MOTHER AND CHILD

The bond between a mother and child is sacred and one you surely do not wish to break. This is especially true in the case of giant monsters. You've probably heard how dangerous it is to get between a bear and its cub, but that is nothing compared to the problems you will have if you separate a giant monster from its baby. Just like in the case of dealing with a bear, a giant monster will lash out violently at anyone who attempts to harm their child. Also, if taken, the mother will be able to use its powerful senses to track down its baby and ensure that it is safely returned to the nest. Don't ever underestimate what a parent will do for its child, even though you regard the monster as a brainless beast.

In case you were stupid enough to actually take a creature back from the lost world when you know full well that it already has a mother, expect some swift and just karma to come and bite you in the butt. As you sit in your home with the new addition to your family, bottle feeding the little creature and wondering if it will grow up someday to find a giant moth, know that somewhere out there, the mother is slowly tromping her way toward your location to reclaim her child. If you happen to survive Mama giant monster coming for her baby and find yourself standing in the smoldering wreckage that was once your home, understand your problems aren't over yet. The authorities will no doubt wish to blame you for the destruction that was caused by bringing the creature to civilization. This means you'll have to pay an enormous amount of restitution for all the damage that was caused and more than likely face jail time to ensure that you actually make good on being able to pay it. Think about all this before you even dream of picking up the little monster and calling him "Stomper."

STOMPER

COSTS

Upkeep on a pet can be very costly and this is especially true when it comes to larger animals. Since you are raising a creature that will someday be 50 feet tall, it is safe to say that you are going to be paying a lot to take care of the basic necessities that come with keeping a creature alive. Just like a pet, you expect the normal expenses such as food and medical costs, but there are other costs that you have to deal with. Due to its size, you are going to need someplace to house the creature, and whenever you feel like taking it somewhere, you are going to need to rent special transportation equipment to move it. If you didn't think about these incidents before, you may want to before you start to venture through the lost civilization hoping to bring home an intact monster egg.

These costs will add up and you may find that you will not be able to raise enough money just by working a day job. In fact, with the amount of time necessary to take care of the creature, you might find it impossible to do both. This is when you need to think about other methods of obtaining money. Contact your local government and begin the process to petition for a grant to take care of the creature. Your overall goal here will be to receive enough grant money so you are able to take care of the creature as a full-time job.

You'll have to start by writing a proposal that describes the problems and costs you will face in taking care of the creature. Make mention that the creature is endangered, which will help you get aid from several different groups that have been set up with the specific intention of preserving rare species. Also in the proposal, you will want to describe how beneficial it will be to have a friendly giant monster around when aliens invade from another planet. There will be a few who will not listen to this idea and try to overturn your proposal. Don't give up, as there will be someone in the government who will see the advantage of raising a small giant creature into a larger one; one that will be able to protect the entire human race if necessary from other world forces who have giant monsters at their disposal.

HOUSING

You won't be able to have the same experiences with a giant monster as you would with other animals that you may own. A perfect example of this is the idea of your pet sleeping in the same bed as you do. Though it may be nice for a dog to curl up at your feet or a cat to sleep on your chest, it is very difficult to share a bed with a giant monster considering the fact that it can easily take up about half the bed with its enormous body. Think of a giant beast, much like a Tyrannosaurus rex but green, with longer arms, a smaller mouth, and some kind of weird accessory on its back if it helps you to visualize what you are dealing with. Now do you actually believe that being is just going to curl into a ball at the foot of your bed? More than likely, this means that the creature will not be able to stay in your home and you will have to find a special place to house it. This will be increasingly difficult depending on whether you live in an urban or a rural area.

It is not as difficult to find a space in an urban area as one might think, if you can find the right place. A large, empty, rundown storage warehouse will serve to give the creature some kind of space to keep it in check during the early years of its life. Just make sure to keep it properly fed and that you chain and lock the entrances shut before you leave the creature alone. The warehouse will essentially serve as a large cage to keep it in and not running loose.

Rural areas are more ideal for raising a monster as they can offer large stretches of land for the creature to run free. The main problem is that you must be the owner of this property to let the creature stay on it. This can be rather costly, especially if you decide that you do not wish the creature to be forced to endure the harsh elements and want some type of coverage for it to go under to stay out of the cold. More than likely, this means that you'll have to build some type of barn for the creature to hide in when it does storm, which is more additional costs. Remember, it might be best to try and find some type of funding when you are trying to keep a monster, as raising it without financial support is next to impossible.

Hopefully, you have received the money from the government issued–grant to afford your own center for the creature. For the purposes of the rest of this chapter, assume that you have already bought your center out in a rural area and named it "The Monster Farm." Let us chronicle what you can expect on the Monster Farm.

DIET

Like all animals, your giant monster is going to need to eat if it wants to survive. Feeding it will not be easy or cheap, with the costs and challenges changing over time in correlation with the three stages of development it may undergo: baby, intermediate, and adulthood.

While it is a baby, you will have the option of feeding it like a baby. In the early stages of development, it will need the food that it would receive from its mother. This means that a bottle full of health drink with some specifically selected nutrition supplements will aid in its growth. Once it is off the bottle, it will be able to eat smaller, more nourishing things. This means that you will have to give it enough food to feed a large dog such as a German Shepherd. Depending on the creature, you may be able to get away with giving it dog food. To help it grow and prepare it for the foods it will eat later on in its growth, a mixture of wet and dry food is recommended. Since there is no proven diet for any giant monsters, you may find yourself going through a trial and error process until you can find a diet that your little monster really enjoys eating.

When your creature reaches the intermediate stage of its development, you'll be faced with a difficult choice: should you continue to feed it yourself and have it rely on you for its meals, or start some interesting training and allow it the opportunity to hunt and forage on its own for food? This is a very difficult choice indeed, considering that either of your choices will result in ramifications when the creature reaches adulthood. If you were to baby it and continue to feed it yourself, you risk the possibility that the creature will start to lose some of its violence and problem-solving skills which it would learn while finding food on its own. Helping your monster in these aspects may make it lack the necessary skill that would be able to help it survive properly in a fight. Remember, the reason you are raising this monster is to have a backup plan in case another monster tries to destroy the world. How good is your backup plan when it immediately starts to run away and cower at the sight of another giant monster?

On the other hand, if you allow the creature to hunt for its food in the intermediate stage when it is a carnivore, you run the risk of it retaining too much violent tendency at an early age. Once the creature has too much of a taste for blood, it may want to continue satisfying the ever- growing craving. This means that after too many kills it may become so ill-tempered and unmanageable that it begins to attack not only your staff, but even you. To prevent this from happening, you want to employ a mixture of the two methods so that the creature is able to understand that it must fend for itself, but can also rely on others for support. Consider having it observe that you are the one that gets its food (food in this case meaning larger animals such as deer or cows that you allow in the area for it to feast on) and secure your post as controller of the food. This will help to ensure that the creature doesn't bite the hand that feeds it.

Upon reaching adulthood, the creature will possess the highest degree of danger to those around it. An adult monster will be large enough to eat an adult male human in just one bite. This would prove to be incredibly dangerous, as your disciplinary measures will only do so much to keep the creature in check and stop it so it does not finish chewing up the victim. Since the creature still has to feed, you will now have to feed it more and allow it to hunt fewer times than before so that you can still enforce your dominant position over the creature. You will just have to give him more room than you ever did previously to ensure there are no casualties.

DOCTOR VISITS

Like any good pet owner, you want to ensure that your creature is healthy at all times. This should not change even though you have a creature that is much larger than some of the other animals that veterinarians are trained for. Due to the immense size and inability to transport the creature without great difficulty, you will instead have to find a vet that not only specializes in large animals but is also willing to make house calls. The vet will come to Monster Farm to make sure that even with his limited amount of information on the creature that he is able to tell that it is growing into healthy adulthood.

This may work for the first few appointments that your monster needs, but down the road, you're going to need something a bit more permanent to take care of it. Eventually, you will want to find a vet who is not only able to take care of your monster but also wishes to employ his or her time and effort into studying the creature as their own personal research project. As the vet proceeds through their research, they will be able to gain insight into how the creature is feeling inside and out as it continues to grow into adulthood. Once they acquire enough information, they will more than likely publish their findings to the rest of the world. This will lead to others being interested in the creature and eventually a new science devoted to the study of other giant creatures will be established. Now you not only furthered the life of the creature by raising it in a safe environment, but at the same time helped the scientific community by offering them a research subject that they were able to study. You have helped the world to not only understand the creature better but created an area of science for future generations.

DISCIPLINE

You'll want to make sure that you have some way of punishing your monster if it steps out of line and does something it shouldn't have. Some of the better examples of bad behavior include eating the neighbor's dog, jumping up and squishing the car, and making multiple attempts to escape from the farm. Such behavior will be unacceptable and you will have to do something to ensure that it doesn't happen again. You won't be able to simply roll up a newspaper and hit it on the nose when it is bad, however, and as the creature gets bigger, it will become harder and harder to discipline it properly. During the infant stage, you will be able to discipline the creature with some type of shock collar or cattle prod. In light of the fact that the creature is about the size of a cow, a cattle prod cannot be looked at as being inhumane as it will have just barely enough of an electrical charge to correct the creature on its inappropriate actions. Also, if the punishment of not allowing the creature to eat dinner is administered, make sure that you do not allow it to eat any small animals or humans that may be in the area as it will no doubt become hungry enough that it decides to just eat anything that walks by. Make sure that you have staff standing by that understand this and don't try to do something as foolish as feeding it under the table, or else you risk the possibility of losing authority you have by controlling its food supply.

As the monster reaches its intermediate phase, it will become even more difficult to discipline its actions. As the creature continues to grow larger and larger, it will be harder for it to recognize you from its tall stature as the one who is in control. You may wish to consider more violent methods of discipline. Understand that under normal circumstances, these disciplinary actions might be considered barbaric, but what you're dealing with here will have a more durable body structure than any other creature you have faced before. Depending on how tall the monster is, you will first want to start with a bullwhip. If that doesn't work, consider investing in some type of industrial-grade cattle prod, one that will be able to give a shock that the creature will truly be able to feel. If such a thing even exists.

As the monster reaches adulthood, disciplining it will become near impossible. You instead have to hope that the lessons you gave it when it was young have affected it to the point that it now has a better understanding of right and wrong. If you are still not 100% sure of the effect that you're parenting skills have had, you may want to consider something drastic: a down switch. A down switch is a device that will be placed at the base of the spine and, when activated, will send a very strong electrical current through the creature's body, incapacitating it. Depending on the restrictions by the government that you have had placed on your giant monster, you may be forced to use a more drastic second option that would work in cooperation with the down switch: a death switch. The death switch will have enough of an electrical current that when pressed will cause the creature's entire nervous system to become damaged beyond the point of repair, rendering it nearly lifeless. Remember that the second option is only for the most hopeless of situations, and depending on what type of guidelines you have in place by your superiors, you may not even have to install it.

Also, make sure you realize that you will not be able to get the creature as riled up as you would with other creatures. Some people who keep large dogs enjoy playing with them and watching them jump around, getting excited over the aspect of play. Be very careful if you actually consider attempting to fill your giant monster with energy, as it could easily backfire. Unlike the large dog owners, you will not be able to simply give the giant monster a scratch behind the ears or a belly rub to calm it down. You will have to find some other way of calming the creature to make sure that once it does get too wound up for its own good, you can keep it docile and stop its wild behavior.

CLEANING UP AFTER IT

One of the most disgusting activities that any pet owner has to deal with is cleaning up their pet's excrement. With many large animals, it can easily become an all-day job cleaning up after them. This is nothing in comparison to what you'll have to deal with.

In the infant phase, the cleaning process will be relatively simple. This should just require a shovel, a wheelbarrow, and someplace to store it. You'll want to have the live-in professor run tests to see if it is possible for the excrement to be used as a type of fertilizer. If you're successful, you'll be able to make some profit off of selling the creature's waste to farmers.

Once the creature reaches its intermediate and adult phases, you will no longer have the option of using just a shovel when you wish to clean up after the creature. More than likely, you'll have to buy some type of heavy-duty construction equipment such as a bulldozer to scoop up the excrement and put it into trucks. The product can then be taken to a distribution center where other farmers can come and pick it up.

When dealing with excrement, understand that there is always the possibility that large intestinal parasites may be swimming around in there. Also, keep in mind that your creature will not have the regular everyday parasites that many animals face in their lifetime. The creature's large body will cause many intestinal parasites that would normally be a smaller size to grow exponentially. This means that something as small as a tapeworm could easily grow to more than ten times its size in the creature's body. This'll mean the average 6-inch tapeworm will eventually become a 60-inch beast, and there's no telling what something like that will do once it leaves the body. For that matter, you will want to make sure that these parasites can't pass through the manure and into the human body. You will not want to be directly responsible for an outbreak of parasites that tear people up. That will just be looked at as bad business.

TRANSPORTATION

There will be some instances when you will have to arrange to transport your baby monster. Whether it's for some type of testing, moving to a new facility, or because you just feel that the big fellow needs a change of scenery, you're going to have to find a way to get it from Point A to Point B without causing a lot of destruction in between. This will be no easy task.

Before you start, you'll want to make sure that you properly sedate the creature before you begin moving it. A creature that is thrashing around too much will endanger not only itself but the people that are transporting it. In the beginning of the monster's development, you should be able to get off relatively easily, using a horse truck or a moving van as it will still be relatively small. Once it has reached its intermediate phase, it will become much more difficult to keep in an enclosed vehicle. Instead, you may have to consider renting a flatbed truck normally used to move houses. These trucks should be durable enough to support the weight of your creature as you move it to its destination.

Unfortunately, once the monster reaches adulthood, you will more than likely not be able to transport it with any type of land vehicle, as it will no longer be able to fit on the roads. Instead, you will have to look into the option of obtaining some air transport to get it where it needs to go. As you sedate the creature, make sure that it falls on some type of large net or other rigging device. Once it is unconscious, you will be able to hook the net to cables that will be connected to a series of helicopters that will lift the creature into the air and transport it to its intended destination. Given the size of the object that you are transporting, you'll want to make sure that you not only have air clearance, but at the same time will want to lift the creature high enough that it does not smash into any high buildings that may be in your flight path. Do not even consider transferring the creature until you have taken all of these factors into consideration.

RAISING A GUARDIAN

The grant proposal you wrote to get the money to afford Monster Farm was issued in the first place so you and your monster might someday save the world. It will not be as easy as simply pointing your monster at the enemy and waiting for it to win. That will instead result in your baby monster losing its life, as it will not be able to handle a truly vicious opponent. You will have to do is to train your monster to be able to fight against other monsters.

While in the infancy stage, you'll want to first train the creature to recognize an opponent. Perhaps consider training the creature to recognize a specific smell that it will instinctively identify as an enemy. At the start of this training, you will want to find someone who can put on protective gear similar to the kind used to train guard dogs. This individual will be your attacker. Spray the equipment with the scent that you are hoping the creature will recognize as an opponent. Once everything is set up, you will want to have the attacker start to harass and assault the creature until it recognizes that this is an enemy that must be dealt with. Eventually, instinct will take over and the creature will go on the offensive. Make sure you that you have some way of stopping the creature, as you don't want your attacker to be harmed.

You may also want to consider the possibility of having your attacker come after you. If you succeeded in establishing yourself as the main food provider and handler for the creature, it will eventually look upon you as a mother figure. When your monster sees that its mother figure is being put in danger, its instinct will once again come into play and it will want to do all it can to protect its mother.

When training is over, make sure that the attacker has properly masked the offending scent so the creature does not try to lunge at him when training is not taking place. With this scent now in the creature's memory, you will be able to perform additional training as the creature develops. As it reaches the intermediate and adults phases, you should set up different types of dummies, coat them in the offending odor, and continue to run training exercises to ensure that the creature is developing its fighting skills.

As long as the training was successful, you will have an easy method of designating a target for the creature to attack. All you will have to do is spray the odor on whatever your monster needs to battle and it will naturally try to take it down. This will ensure that the earth has some form of protection against the appearance of an unwanted giant monster.

NATURE VS. NURTURE

The idea of nature versus nurture has been debated between psychologists for centuries. The idea comes from two very different principles of the mind: nature which focuses on ideas and behaviors that are ingrained within us from the start, and nurture, which focuses on the idea, that with the proper amount of outside lessons, natural behavior can be corrected. This argument will heavily come into play as you start to raise your giant monster and the resulting case study will help provide an excellent example to whichever one of the arguments doesn't prove to shine through.

Since you have decided to take on the burden of raising a giant monster, you'll be working to fight against the nature side of the argument. In this case, the nature side states that your monster is a monster and will be nothing more. There is no hope of changing it, as it was made to destroy cities and trample people under its feet. Siding with the nature argument, though, dictates that it would be much easier just to kill the creature and be done with it, not running the risk of it following nature's course and growing up to be a destroyer.

Due to the fact that you decided to go through the effort of raising the monster, you have decided to side with the idea of nurture. You are hoping that with proper discipline and direction, your little monster will grow up to fight against other monsters without the risk of it devouring human beings. This is going to be a very hard fact to prove, though, as your monster is still an animal. It relies on instincts more than thoughts when dealing with the many problems it faces on a regular basis.

It will be up to you to train your monster to the point that he recognizes that humans are friendly and are not tasty treats for him to consume. One of the best ways to enforce this idea is to make sure that you creature never goes hungry, as it will begin to sniff around humans with an interest in what they taste like. If the creature slips up even once and does consume a human, all your efforts would unfortunately be in vain. Once the creature has a taste for humans, there'll be little that you'll be able to do other than perhaps administer some degree of shock treatment. Also, any creature that has attacked a human being of its own accord is mandated by law to be put down, as it is a threat to humans everywhere. Considering the creature in question, this will be without a doubt true.

THE MONSTER WHISPERER

Many people throughout the world have unique connections with animals. There are even those who believe they have such a special bond with animals that they can communicate with them on a personal level. In the many volunteers that apply, hoping to work with your monster (and there will be a LOT given the unique nature of your program), at least one of them will be under the explicit belief that they have the ability to communicate with the monster. Do not dismiss this individual's claims as being false or, for that matter, call the proper authorities to see if it's possible to have them observed at a mental health facility. Instead, hire them on a temporary basis and see if their claims are true. If they are, you'll be granted a golden opportunity to get in touch with the monster in ways you never thought possible.

An individual who is blessed with the ability to talk and understand a creature so big is a rare gift indeed. A screening process will be able to help filter out those who are obviously lying about their gift. If by chance you do find someone who possesses the ability, it will become of great aid as you progress in your research. A monster whisperer will be able to help the creature to understand ideas and concepts it would normally have some difficulty comprehending. The individual can also act as a calming agent to help settle the creature down when it starts to get out of hand. This will help to make sure that there are no instances of escape because the creature will be told the farm is its home. It will also ensure that no excessive amount of force is needed to stop the creature if its behavior becomes too wild.

You also want to consider how receptive the creature is toward the idea of others singing for it. As mentioned in the counterattack section, beasts can be easily susceptible to the songs that humans sing and find them to be a very soothing force in their life. Experimenting with singing will be one of the first steps you will want to take as you begin to raise your creature. Still, there are some aspects of singing that will be unable to be recorded by modern technology; a type of energy that the creature feels as someone sings a song to calm it down. This energy will be essential, as it will help to get the creature under control and put it at ease. You will wish to find someone who possesses the ability to give off the energy the creature particularly enjoys.

BREEDING

How successful your program is, how well the creature performs as a guardian, and how much the world is under constant attack by renegade giant monsters will all be determining the factors in determining its longevity. If your program does continue, the idea to have a second creature around might be suggested. If you're up for the challenge and are granted enough additional funds to be able to afford it, then this might not be a bad idea.

You will want to start off by finding another egg. You'll achieve this by making a voyage back to the lost civilization where the first egg was found. Once the egg is secured, you'll want to make sure that it is raised at the same level that your previous monster was to make sure that you obtain the same results. You'll eventually have to wait until the second monster has gone through puberty before you consider the option of allowing the two to mate. You want to make sure that the two creatures have some type of interaction before the time comes for breeding. This initial interaction will make sure that the two creatures actually get along and will ensure that there will be no complications in behavior when the time comes for mating. The more they like each other, the easier it will be to get the two of them to fornicate.

If the two creatures refuse to fornicate, you will still have options at your disposal. One possibility will be in-vitro fertilization. Simply extract some of the male monster's sperm and use it to fertilize some of the female monster's eggs. This will help to ensure that things are done correctly. Depending on how much lab work is done, you may wish to modify some monstrous characteristics through gene engineering so the child is stronger and faster than its parents were. Be careful with this practice, as you do not want to engineer a creature that you will not be able to control.

Unfortunately, the breeding process is not without its complications. Once you add more animalistic and natural instincts back into the equation, you are setting yourself up to deal with a lot of headaches. One of the first points made in this chapter was that it was a very bad idea to even consider the idea of separating a mother from its child. Well, you will now be faced with the option of having to do just that if you wish to facilitate that the newborn creature undergoes that same training and discipline that its parents did. You could try seeing if the parents understand and the teachings of becoming a guardian have been engraved in their personalities.

Regrettably, you may not be blessed with having this option when raising your newborn monster. Your superiors may wish to ensure that the creature has exactly the same upbringing as its parents had to ensure that a new guardian is born exactly the way they say it is. Your facility will be faced with the sad realization that you will have to separate parent from child. Though this can be hard for you as the caregiver to both parents, understand it is for the greater good of humanity, and just make sure that the newborn will receive as much love and care as you previously gave.

REINTRODUCING TO THE WILD

Here is a hypothetical situation. Say that you are not successful in raising your giant monster. Perhaps you find the process is too much stress or that it is holding you back from pursuing some of your other passions. Maybe the creature itself is not adapting to modern civilization and the only course of action is to have it returned to the environment that will be able to handle its presence. If the creature originally came from a lost civilization or some island where giant creatures still exist, then you'll have the option of being able to send it back into the wild. Once you are able to arrange some form of transport, you'll be able to take the creature back to a home that will be able to properly sustain its existence.

Understand that returning the monster is not as simple as just dropping it off and leaving. You will want to establish some way of being able to monitor the monster to ensure that it is successfully adapting to its new home. Hopefully, the research scientist you were working with has had a degree of success studying the creature and now wishes to further their research. In a safe area, the two of you will be able to set up some type of camp to properly monitor and record your monster's reintroduction into the lost civilization. With any luck, it will find its place, learn to hunt, and hopefully find a mate to procreate with. If that doesn't work, you may want to consider the option of staging an intervention on his behalf if you are truly willing to risk your life for the creature. What you want to do is get close to another one of his kind and become its prey. As long as the creature you raised still recognizes you as the one who gave it food, it will still possess a natural instinct to protect and repay your kindness. This will cause it to go on the attack, fight with the creature, and hopefully win, carving out his own place in this mysterious world. You'll of course want to make sure that you exercise some degree of safety precaution to make sure that you don't get yourself killed. Consider having some type of tranquilizer gun around to make sure the predator goes down if your creature arrives too late. Though this is questionable unethical, understand that it is for your baby monster's own good.

THE DON'T LIST

The following is a list of suggestions you want to make sure that you follow if you have any hope whatsoever of succeeding in being the caretaker of a giant monster. Understand that these cautionary measures are in place to ensure your safety and are not intended to rain on your parade. There are simple guidelines that you must follow to make sure that you don't get yourself killed trying to keep a monster as a household pet. This guide has always been about ensuring that people are able to survive any encounter that they face with monsters and nothing less.

1. Don't adopt a nuclear monster. It is natural to feel sym–

pathy for a creature that has undergone some type of nuclear or atomic experimentation, but the fact is that you will be unable to take care of it properly without risking severe physical health issues to yourself and others. By taking in a creature that has in the past experienced such experiments, you run the risk that the creature radiates at some level. Prolonged exposure to this type of creature will result in a failure in your physical health. You'd only be able to keep a nuclear creature if you had access to a high-end facility that was insulated to prevent the creature from attacking others. Even then, you'll still have to make sure that you are always wearing a hazmat suit and undergo decontamination after each time you find yourself around the creature. If you are without these resources and materials, it is best just to leave the creature alone, as there is nothing you'll be able to do to help it.

   2. Don't let it roam free. With many animals, even not highly trained ones, many people simply let them outside to do their business and assume they will return home when they wish to be let inside. Unfortunately, you will not have this option when you're raising a giant monster. Even if you are able to train it to always come home after it runs free and does its business, understand that every time it walks, it will cause damage. There's no telling how far it could go or where it could wander. For all you know, it can easily make its way into a city and create a GME without realizing it. If you have to let it out of whatever barn or large cage that houses it, you may wish to consider the option of fencing off your entire property with some type of industrial fencing material. Consider titanium beams for a start, and then see if you can run some type of electrical wire through them. That way once you do let the creature out, it will be able to run around freely on your property yet receive a nasty electrical shock if it tries to roam too far. Make sure you place proper signs at the front gate of your property to warn anyone who might casually arrive that they are in danger if they touch the fence. The last thing you want is some girl scout who's coming by to sell cookies being thrown back a few hundred yards due to electrical shock.

   On the same note, you may want to consider constructing an invisible fence. This might actually save you some money because you will no longer have to buy all the building materials for the fence. An invisible fence is a type of electric collar that shocks the animal if it goes too far past a sensor and will be helpful in making sure that your monster doesn't wind up on the news with helicopters reporting on the destruction it is inflicting on the city. If you go with this option, though, you want to make sure you buy a collar that can give enough of an electrical shock that it can set the creature right. If the shock is too weak, it may not get through the creature's thick skin and cause it to just continue on like nothing happened. Keep this in mind before you go out and do your shopping. Also, make sure to derive some type of emergency generator in case of a storm and power goes out. You don't want the only safety net keeping the monster from going on a rampage to just disappear.

3. Don't let it eat anyone. Through a mixture of proper discipline and diet management, you'll be able to ensure that the creature does not find itself to be hungry to the point that it decides it needs to eat a human being. Nothing will cause your research grant to be pulled quicker than a detailed progress report listing how many of your workers were lost to the creature and how much money has been paid in compensations to the victims' families. Also, depending on the situation and who is placed in charge of overseeing the Monster Farm, problems could arise with the monster accidentally attacking an individual thinking that its food. If your supervisors are too forceful, they will more than likely immediately insist that the creature be put down to ensure that it does not pose any type of threat to humans that are around it. To prevent this from happening, make sure that you maintain a strict discipline and diet regiment to keep the chances of human snacking low.

4. Don't play too rough. Some people who own larger animals play a little rougher because they assume their pet will be able to handle it. For example, they may play tug-of-war with their dog using an old sock. This probably won't be as advisable when it comes to playing with a giant monster. Say, for example you getting out a rope and attempting to play tug of war with your monster just like a dog owner would enjoy doing. With the rope in his mouth, the monster could easily swing you around or, if you're holding on too tight, potentially rip one of your limbs off. Make sure that you are prepared for this kind of occurrences before you even think about playing. You may need to wear protective equipment to make sure that you are able to survive if play gets too rough.

5. Don't threaten anyone with your monster. Your giant monster is not a weapon except when expected to fend off other giant monsters that may potentially harm human beings. Threatening other individuals with your giant monster like it was some kind of tool for your own personal use is wrong. If some neighbor doesn't like you and goes out of their way to show it, you cannot turn around and threaten to use your giant monster to destroy their home. This will not only serve to escalate tension between you and your neighbor, but also might lead to your neighbor calling the authorities on you, resulting in you receiving a fine for threatening a person with a giant monster at the very least. A giant monster is a responsibility, not a right. It is up to you to step up to the plate and display a maturity that others might not be able to have. Keep that in mind before you "accidentally" forget to turn on the invisible fence one night and watch as your giant monster steps on your neighbor's car.

6. Don't coddle it. Since the creature will more than likely be your primary concern, it is going to take up a lot of your life. At times, you might even feel like addressing it as your baby, but it is not a baby at all. Special treatment and giving it treats at times will eventually lead to it becoming soft. You cannot let your monster lose all of its nerve, as it may someday have to defend the entire world from invading forces. It will do no good to throw a very large baby who runs away and cries to its mother into a fight. Make sure that the creature still retains some amount of fight or you risk the possibility of hurting the creature in the long run when it is eventually forced to fend off some alien invasion. Without some level of fighting instinct, the creature will more than likely get itself killed because it is not vicious enough to stand toe to toe with the aliens.

Chapter 5:
REAL LIFE
GIANT
MONSTERS

Many of the creatures mentioned in this book have yet to make their appearances known to the world except in literature and film. Still, there are creatures of considerable size and strength that already exist. Some of these creatures are friendly, others deadly, and one is one of the greatest mysteries on the planet. Even though many of these creatures are friendly, it is still helpful to have information on them so that you are prepared in the result that something unforeseen happens, such as a mutation. An already large creature getting even bigger is never a good thing.

Name: Ostrich (Struhio Camelus)
Locations: Various parts of Africa
Height: 6-9 ft.
Weight: 140-290 lbs.
Diet: Plants and insects
Species Status: Low, but not endangered
Danger Level: Low, unless intimidated

About: The largest flightless bird on the planet, the ostrich makes up for its inability to fly by being incredibly fast on the ground. The speed of the ostrich is so well known that in some corners of the world they are raced. These creatures possess a gentle nature and for the most part are not threatening in nature despite their enormous size. Consisting on a diet of primarily plants with the occasional insect, these creatures pose no immediate threat to a human.

Recommendation: Even though these creatures are non-threatening by nature, they still have ways to defend themselves if provoked. Their long legs enable them to deliver an incredibly powerful kick that could potentially kill a person if they were hit too hard. This will only occur as a defensive mechanism, so it is best just to leave these creatures as is and not risk aggravating them in any way.

Name: Whale Shark (Rhincondon Typus)
Locations: Tropical Seas
Height: 18-32 ft.
Weight: 18-22 tons
Diet: Plankton
Species Status: Low, but not endangered
Danger Level: Low

About: The largest fish in the world is probably one of the gentlest. Although it has a way of wanting to eat sea plants and small fish that it scoops up, it poses absolutely no danger to humans. If by chance you are still afraid of their massive size, then stay away from the coasts of Australia during the spring, as they tend to use this area in their migration.

Recommendation: For the creature to pose any threat, you would have to be on the water in the first place. For a creature of this size to come onto the land, a massive mutation will take place to change it and give it the option of ground mobility. Even if it does find some way to gain the ability to move on the land, it still does not have the ability to breathe on it and will die soon after taking its first steps on land.

The only way that a human could even find themselves having difficulty with these creatures is if they tried to capture one. Moving something that weighs more than 20 tons is no easy task. Better just leave them in their place and not have to worry about trying to drag them out of the water.

Name: Blue Whale (Balaenoptera musculus)

Locations: There are few parts of the ocean that the blue whale won't swim in. For the most part, as long there is enough room for their large bodies to fit they will move through it.

Height: 75-100 ft.

Weight: 110-120 tons

Diet: Plankton and small fish

Species Status: Low, but not endangered

Danger Level: Low

About: The largest creature on the planet, the blue whale swims the oceans as far as its large body will allow. The whales' non-threatening nature and soft diet has caused it to receive the nickname of "gentle giants of the sea." This non-threatening nature has proven to be their own downfall, as to this day the species is still targeted by whaling fleets hoping to capture and kill the creature.

Recommendation: Again, just like the whale shark, the blue whale will pose no threat as long as you are on land and are not attempting to capture it or interfere with its movement. At the same time, due to their large size, it is best not to get them confused and cause them to go out of control. What many people don't realize is that using sonar in the general area of the blue whale throws its senses out of balance, causing it to thrash about in confusion. If by chance you are on a ship and caught up in the confusion of a thrashing blue whale, then you may find yourself in trouble.

Name: Anaconda (Eunectes Murinus)
Locations: Jungles of South America
Height: 27–30 ft.
Weight: 550 lbs.
Diet: Pigs, deer, capybara, etc.
Species Status: Not threatened
Danger Level: High

About: Probably the second-deadliest creature on this list, the anaconda is a force to be feared. Their preferred form of attack is winding itself around their prey and squeezing the air out of them until they stop fighting. The anaconda can then consume the creature and begin the slow digestive process. Thanks to their properly formed jaw these creatures can fit a large amount in their bodies. Stay clear of them if at all possible.

Recommendation: Stay on the land for the most part as these snakes are exceptionally good swimmers and would have little difficulty picking off someone in the water if they were hungry enough. That being said, it's probably a better idea just to stay away from them at all, as there's no telling how quickly the creature could snap at you.

If by chance you are captured in their squeezing grasp, there is unfortunately little that you'll be able to do to get out of it. By being trapped in its coils, the creature will eliminate your ability to use your arms to reach for any type of weapon or device you might have that could help you. At best, in the limited time you'll have as the creature starts to crush the air out of you, you'll be able to reach into your pocket to try to find something to assist you in your time of need, but the likelihood of finding anything of particular worth in your pocket is highly unlikely. Again, keeping your distance from your creature is highly recommended if you plan on growing any older in the near future.

Name: Goliath Bird Eater Spider (Theraphosa blondi)
Locations: Northern South America
Height: 1 ft.
Weight: 6 oz.
Diet: Insects and small birds
Species Status: Low risk of endangerment
Danger Level: Low (surprisingly)

About: The largest spider on the planet and a member of the tarantula family, the Goliath Bird Eater Spider surprisingly poses very little threat to humans. The truth is that these creatures do not possess enough venom to be able to do any real damage to humans and would usually only bite one in self-defense. The creature does possess the ability to kick urticating bristles from their body at their prey, but this will only be more of an annoyance to humans than an actual threat.

Recommendation: In previous chapters, the fact was pointed out that when facing down a giant spider, one of the biggest difficulties you will have to overcome is the fact that its appearance is mostly unpleasant to many people. This holds true with the Goliath Bird

Eater, and if you happen to encounter one, its repulsive appearance will more than likely cause an individual to become uncomfortable. Do your best to remember that these creatures pose no threat to humans and avoid backing them into a corner to the point that they feel threatened and see a need to be defensive. Just leave them alone and they'll leave you alone—plain and simple.

Name: Giant Squid
Locations: Oceans all over the world
Height: 43 ft.
Weight: 1 ton
Diet: Fish
Species Status: Not threatened
Danger Level: Medium (its location makes it less threatening)

About: Thanks primarily to the fact these creatures live in the deepest areas of the ocean, information on them has been difficult to gather over the years. This means any information that we do know is based primarily on the few specimens that have been harvested over the years. From what has been studied, we know that their tentacles reach up to 16 feet, meaning they would easily be able to wrap around a person, if need be. Thanks to ancient myths of the sea, this creature has the reputation of popping out and dragging sailors to their death. Like many squids, they are blessed with the ability to produce ink as a camouflage technique to get away from anything that threatens it.

Recommendation: If the giant squid lived closer to the surface of the water, then the threat it poses to human beings would be far greater. Luckily for humans, this creature tends to stay in the deepest oceans and not come up very often. In all likelihood, you would have to be on some type of deep-sea exploration to even have a chance of encountering these creatures. If by chance you are captured in the squid's tentacles, do your best to fight it off. Try and aim for its eye as it has the largest eyes in the world (10 inches in diameter). Just stick a knife in there or fire in a harpoon and it will moan in pain. Unfortunately, when it does, it will shoot its ink, which may make it hard to tell where you're swimming.

Name: Saltwater Crocodile (Crocodylus Porosus)
Locations: Southern Asia and Australia
Height: 17 ft.
Weight: 1 ton
Diet: Monkeys, wild boars, and people
Species Status: Low risk of endangerment
Danger Level: High

About: One of the most dangerous known giant monsters on this earth is the saltwater crocodile. Waiting patiently at the water's edge for its prey to come, a saltwater crocodile will use the thrashing of its large tail for propulsion as it reaches up to grab its prey and pull it under the water to drown it. Given their size and their carnivorous nature, they would not hesitate to attack a human that got too close to their area.

Recommendation: If you are in an area where the saltwater crocodile is known to live, then by all means, exercise extreme caution and stay far away from the water. If you are grabbed by the creature and pulled underwater, you will have precious little time to escape, so listen very closely. When dragged under, grab something in your pocket like a pen with a sharp, pointed edge and jam it into the creature's eye socket. Hopefully, this will give you the distraction you're hoping for to get the creature to release its grasp on you and give you the ability to swim to the shore. This is easier said than done, so to be on the safe side, stay as far away from the water as possible.

Name: Chinese Giant Salamander (Andrias davidianus)
Locations: China
Height: 6 ft.
Weight: 100–110 lbs.
Diet: Crabs and shrimp
Species Status: Highly endangered
Danger Level: Low

About: The largest salamander in the world, these creatures pose little threat to human beings. This is due primarily to the fact that there simply aren't that many Chinese giant salamanders left in the world. Thanks to environmental changes and pollution, food stores for these creatures have run low, resulting in their slow deterioration as a species. Its body's use as both a delicacy and in the field of medicine have also helped in its decline.

Recommendation: If you do find yourself facing down these creatures, afraid for some reason that it might attack you, you'll want to take advantage of the fact that it has very poor eyesight. Since it depends on detecting vibrations through sensory nodes on its body, all you really need to do is stand still to avoid detection. Once it believes you are not there, you'll be given the opportunity to escape from the situation. Don't go after it for its worth as a delicacy. The poor species already has enough problems without everyone in the world discovering how delicious it is.

Name: Cinereous Vulture (Aegypius monachus)
Locations: Europe and Asia
Height: 10 ft. (wingspan)
Weight: 15–31 lbs.
Diet: Carcasses
Species Status: Endangered
Danger Level: High

About: The largest birds in the Bird of Prey families, these scavengers subsist primarily on the dead remains of different animals. This means that they do not move in on a target until it begins to give off the smell of death, which attracts them like bees to honey. Thanks to their large wingspans, they are able to fly to great heights before swooping down to finish off their prey when they are at their weakest. With the use of its powerful beak, it is able to rip its meals apart in seconds as it begins to feast on them. Do your best to stay off their menu by staying alive at all costs.

Recommendation: If you find yourself faced with a large Cinereous vulture circling overhead, it more than likely means that you are on the verge of dying. You want to take two actions to ensure that you will not become this creature's next meal. The first step is to get some food and make sure that you fill yourself up enough that you don't pass out on the ground and give the vulture an opportunity to swoop in and start to eat you. Once you have nourished yourself, your next course of action would be to find some type of masking scent to cover up the smell that was attracting the vulture to begin with. This will throw the bird off and help it to lose track of you. Don't be so quick to celebrate right away, as this creature's sense of smell allows it to smell prey at least a mile away. You will want to make sure you not only have a potent scent to cover your own, but also that you are well out of range before you wash it off. Just make sure to get out of the situation that caused you to starve and that will prevent the creature from coming back in the near future.

Name: Loch Ness Monster
Locations: Loch Ness, Highlands, Scotland
Height: Unknown
Weight: Unknown
Diet: Unknown, presumably fish
Species Status: Endangered/Extinct (By all accounts, the creature is assumed to be the last of its kind. Some scientists and researchers have conducted studies which lead to the conclusion that the creature is dead.)
Danger Level: Low (Throughout the history of the creature, there has never been a single report that it has actually attacked a person. It's safe to write it off as friendly as long as it is not antagonized.)

About: The Loch Ness Monster is a modern-day wonder and one of the true giant monsters of this planet today. First reported back on May 2, 1933 by a journalist, the creature has reportedly been cited numerous times to this very day in and around Loch Ness. Its tendency to always stay in this general area has resulted in it receiving the nicknames "Loch Ness Monster" or "Nessie."

Through the limited (and poor quality) images that exist of the creature, it has been hypothesized that it is more than likely some type of Plesiosaur. The Plesiosaur, a type of dinosaur that existed at the end of the last era of dinosaurs (the Cretaceous period), was a water-based creature that had a long neck and dieted mostly on fish and other types of water creatures. It has been theorized that the creature and its ancestors were able to survive the E.L.E. (Extinction Level Event) by hiding in underwater caves that are around the loch.

Recommendation: If you find yourself in the Highlands of Scotland and by some incredible circumstance are face to face with this legendary creature, there is only one course of action to take: photograph it as much as humanly possible. Congratulations, as you have stumbled on one of the greatest mysteries and elusive creatures ever to walk the earth! You will want to make sure you take many pictures of the creature before it slips away. In the past, individuals who have encountered the creature have only been able to take one or two shots of inferior quality, so make sure that the flash is on and your thumb is not obscuring the lens as you take as many pictures as possible to prove the creature's existence to the world.

Also, since the creature has no known incidents of attacking humans, you will for the most part be safe as long as you stay out of the way and do not antagonize it. This means you will want to ignore that part of your brain that is telling you to climb up on the back of the creature so that your good friend can take a photo of you to post on the internet. This is highly unadvised and one of the biggest mistakes people make when dealing with giant monsters. Reckless behavior of this matter will get individuals killed, so think smart and you should be fine.

Chapter 6:
THE REVIEW
SECTION

Now that you have studied all the materials necessary for surviving a giant monster attack, it's time to see if you have actually been able to retain any of it.

THE CHECKLIST:

Does your GME-Kit (Giant Monster Event Kit) include the following?

- Flares

- A cell phone

- Dog repellent

- An Audio Recording Device

- Camera

- Water and light provisions

- Flashlight

- First Aid Kit

- A change of clothes

THE QUIZ

The following is a simple quiz to see if you truly have memorized all the information that is in this book. Remember, it's okay if you don't remember all of it; it's not like it's life-saving advice that will someday ensure that you are able to survive unspeakable levels of destruction or anything. An answer key is provided for you at the end of the chapter.

1. When facing an atomic monster, which of the following is something that is NOT useful for the situation?

    a. A hazmat suit

    b. Radiation Shielding

    c. A nuclear bomb

2. If the creature possesses some type of projectile weapon, should you think of escaping in a plane?

    a. Yes

    b. No

3. A giant spider has spun a large web and you find yourself caught in it with a handy lighter. Should you light the web on fire?

a. Yes

b. No

4. Which of the following are great ways to deal with a Tyrannosaurus rex?

a. Stay perfectly still

b. Lure it to a low-temperature area

c. Use large quantities of tranquilizer darts

d. All of the above

5. Which of the following is better to use against a giant grasshopper?

a. A flamethrower

b. A gas bomb

6. You have discovered a hole leading down into the creature's lair. Do you investigate it?

a. Yes

b. No

7. The following are good ways of dealing with a giant robot except for one. Which?

a. Infecting it with a computer virus

b. Using water to short out its circuits

c. Overloading it with electricity

d. Firing off an electromagnetic pulse

e. Trick question. All are good answers.

8. A giant squid is destroying a large number of shipping vessels in a certain part of the ocean. Should you use the information provided in this book to go out and try to kill the creature to claim the reward money?

a. Yes

b. No

9. Which of the following is the best scientific method for dealing with a giant monster?

a. Cloning the monster

b. A gas bomb

c. A giant robot

10. You have discovered the identity of the individual that a Cosmic Being is inhabiting. Do you...?

a. Alert the media of who they are

b. Blackmail the person, saying you'll tell the world otherwise

c. Introduce yourself to the person and ask them if there is anything you can do to help them in their fight

11. You have discovered a giant monster's nest and there are unhatched monster eggs inside. What is the first thing you should do?

a. Grab one of the eggs and run

b. Make sure that mother is around

c. Destroy the eggs just to be on the safe side

12. What is the danger level that an anaconda possesses?

a. Low

b. Medium

c. High

ESSAY QUESTIONS:

You have discovered that the rampaging giant bird from outer space is being controlled remotely. What do you do?

_____

_____

_____

_____

_____

_____

_____

_____

_____

_____

A mysterious cult hopes to awaken their dark god. What can you do to make sure that they are unsuccessful?

_____

_____

_____

_____

_____

_____

_____

_____

_____

_____

You hope to attack a dragon that is lying dormant after laying siege to the city, but find that it's being protected by a group of protesters who insist that "Dragons are people too." If you still wish to carry out the attack, what is the best plan of action for this situation?

_____

_____

_____

_____

_____

_____

_____

_____

_____

_____

ANSWER KEY:

1. C. You already have enough radiation in the equation. Using any more will only result in bad things happening, like the creature growing even stronger than if presently is.

2. No. A monster with a projectile weapon will easily pick off a plane from the sky. It's better to find deep cover and drive in a ground vehicle that does not draw a lot of attention.

3. No. You have no way of controlling how the flames will spread. Lighting the web on fire will only result in creating a problem that's just as bad as the uncontrollable giant spider.

4. D. All of the above. All of the ways mentioned will help

you to make sure that you are not the T-rex's next meal.

5. A. A flamethrower will pose fewer hazards to those around you, so long as you have a way of keeping the fire under control. When you use the flamethrower, make absolutely sure that you kill the grasshopper so it doesn't hop off and spread the flames.

6. No. You never want to try to engage a monster on its home turf. If anything, you need to find a way to lure the creature out into the open so that it has no possible way of using the environment to its advantage.

7. B. An advance robot system will be properly insulated to the point its system will be unaffected by water damage. Make sure to keep this in mind when you try to take it down.

8. No. Above all else when dealing with sea monsters, if you have the option of staying away from the water then by all means you should be doing so. The main purpose of this handbook is to keep you alive, not make you rich.

9. C. Cloning is never a good idea and you usually need far too much gas to be able to properly incapacitate a target. Building a robot that will be able to take down your target is probably the safest idea when looking at a scientific device to use against the creature.

10. C. The Cosmic Being is going to have enough trouble battling whatever monster has come trying to destroy the earth. You need to try and do everything in your power to see if you can help them with their task.

11. B. The other two possibilities will only result in you being killed by the mother monster for messing with her children. Making a mother monster unhappy is a very bad idea.

12. C. An anaconda is a very dangerous creature. You want to make absolutely sure that you don't get anywhere near them as it could result in you being their next meal.

ESSAY QUESTIONS:

1. You should have made some mention in your essay of isolating, copying, and analyzing the signal so you are able to use it to take control of the giant bird.

2. Your essay should make sure to mention something along the lines of disrupting their ritual to stop the creature from being able to rise from its eternal sleep.

3. With the protesters in your way, you're going to want to try and attack from a distance. This means that you will probably want to think of about using some type of sniper rifle that comes equipped with ammunition powerful enough to destroy the creature in just one hit. Just make sure that it doesn't explode in a way that causes so much damage that the protesters are hurt as a result.

Chapter 7:
CONGRATULATIONS! YOU SURVIVED!

If you have made it this far, then congratulations. You have survived a giant monster attack and should be rewarded for it. Take the time to grab yourself a pizza or maybe an ice cream cone before you return to the arduous task of rebuilding your house after it was destroyed by a giant mutated bunny. You can now take satisfaction in the fact that you were prepared for a giant monster to attack your town and had the proper information necessary to ensure that you could not only survive, but at the same time stage a counter attack.

Don't get too cocky, though. Just because you were able to survive this attack doesn't mean that you will survive them all. Who knows? The very next day, you could find yourself under attack of a giant lobster sent down from some planet on the other side of the solar system.

The World after monsters
Of course, you realize that after a major earth-shattering event takes place (and it's safe to say that once any of the giant monsters that have been listed in this book appear, you can consider it an Earth-shattering Event), the world we all know and love will have changed. It may be for good or may be for bad, depending on what happens in the world after the monsters show their ugly faces. Still, life after the monsters are destroyed is just as important as preparing for when they do appear.

Clean up
Way to go! You killed the giant monster that was rampaging through the city bent on destroying all mankind. Unfortunately, there is still one large problem you have to deal with: disposing of your fallen opponent's corpse.

What? Were you thinking you would just leave it there and let nature take its course? Let's think about that for just a second. Have you ever seen a dead animal on the side of the road or the woods? Do you know what happens after a while to the body of that fallen creature? It becomes a buffet for every scavenger around from hungry dogs to insects looking to use the place as a nesting ground for a litter of unborn maggots. Now times that by about a hundred, and you will have a reasonable idea of what you are going to be dealing with if you end up leaving that fallen giant monster in the middle of the city without properly disposing of it. Here are a few ideas on how you can get rid of that eyesore with minimal difficulty.

Cremation

What's a better send-off for a being that was a mighty opponent and gave you the fight of your life than to burn its body like the warriors of ancient times? None come close to being as symbolic as covering the monster's skin with a flammable liquid and then setting it on fire. The flames will burn intensely to the point that they give the giant monster the proper departure it deserves.

Two notes on this plan, though. First, you will want to conduct an analysis on the creature to ensure that burning it doesn't cause some harmful chemicals to release into the atmosphere, resulting in damage that would be just as destructive as the creature was but in a much more devastating way in the long run. Second, if you do end up going with the fire, it is essential that you exercise the proper fire safety protocols. You'll more than likely want to coordinate with your local fire department and fire departments from neighboring towns. Just to be on the safe side in case it does go out of control, it might be a better idea to just put the entire state on alert before you light the first match.

A barbeque

After you get back the tests and see that burning the creature will not cause harmful effects to people or the environment, have the scientist run a few more tests and see what would happen if a person were to eat the creature. Although there are a lot of you out there that might find this to be a more barbaric practice, let's look at this in a sensible light. This is a lot of meat we are talking about here, and there is a good chance that there will be a lot of hungry and tired people who may now not have access to the food supplies they previously had before the giant monster attack. What better way for the creature to give back to the community than to allow itself to be served as a meal for all the victims of its attack? The creature, if processed properly, will not only be able to feed the people in the area but also help a lot of people until the proper services can get back into action. Just make sure you process the creature in a timely manner so as not to risk it going bad. It already caused enough trouble; you don't want it to exact a form of revenge from beyond the grave by giving the citizens a major case of food poisoning.

One huge grave

There are some moments during and after the GME when you are going to have to look at situations and places and truly consider if they are really worth rebuilding. If the monster was killed in a major city, think of everything you will have to rebuild. First, you are going to have to dispose of the body, then start rebuilding, and finally dedicate a large portion of the new city to be some type of memorial to all the people who were lost in the wake of the attack. Why not just eliminate the middleman and turn the entire city into one mass grave for the creature and memorial for all who have died? It's pretty simple, really: just set some charges underneath the city that will cause the corpse to fall along with a large amount of rubble and discarded buildings. From there, simply pave over, get some statues ordered, set up some kind of eternal flame, and BOOM! You have turned the city into a constant reminder of the dangers that can occur during a GME. Make sure to pay your respects to those who have passed before going on with the rest of the rebuilding process.

Burial at sea

Much like sailors back in the day, when a body is gone, it's sometimes best to simply drop it into the sea and let the fish take care of the rest. This is also a way of dealing with that giant monster's corpse that is giving you so much trouble. Just get some suspension cable and a few military helicopters together and fly the dead beast out to sea. Ensure that they all release their lines at the same time, though, or risk one of them being dragged under by the weight of the creature.

This is another one of those cases where you want to ensure that you have run the necessary tests on the creature's body. Though the fish and bacteria will cause the creature to erode over time, the fact is that if there is something harmful in the creature's body, there is no telling how much damage it will do to the local environment. If the body is riddled with toxins, you have just essentially poisoned a few million fish, and there is no way to properly monitor every fishing boat coming into port with their catch of the day. Before you know it, these infected fish will wind up at the local seafood restaurant and cause a massive wave of food poisoning. To repeat: the object of the clean-up process is to NOT give a large population of people indigestion.

Recycling

This is more in regards to the giant robots, but there are a lot of other uses a person could have for some of the pieces of the dead monster. With the robots, if you are able to find a way to break them down and use their pieces to help service the people that were harmed in the GME, then by all means do. Whether it's to use its armor for a wall in someone's house or turn its helmet into some type of fancy specialty restaurant, the idea is that you are trying to find a way to use the material so that it doesn't just end up in a landfill. There is already going to be enough garbage around thanks to all the pieces of building that will have to be cleared away to start the rebuilding process that trying to use the monster for some good would be a valuable service to the community. Also, remember that if the robot had any advanced technology, you need to get someone on reverse engineering so it can be of benefit to humanity. If there is some way to turn the situation around into a positive, then you have to look for it, even in the rubble of a GME.

Paranoia

If you thought you were alone before in believing your giant monster theories, know that you will have no need to look for people to talk with after the GME takes place. Everyone from the most respectable newscaster to the guy you see every day on your way into work will be willing to discuss giant monsters with you. Unfortunately, just because everyone is on board with it doesn't mean you will meet with the cream of the crop in this new trend.

You will soon find that the crazy ones have decided to get on board with discussing when and where the next GME will take place. Well, the crazy ones appeared before but now they are going to be coming out in droves after there are giant footprints in the pavement and people start taking selfies with them. It will be the next biggest thing since planking. To ensure that you don't get surrounded with too many nut bars, it will probably be a good idea to gather a group of trusted individuals around you, each with their own skill and trait to bring to the team. Once you channel your skills together, you will be able to be on the ball for the next GME that takes place.

Opportunists

People are always trying to make a quick buck. This fact will not change just because a GME has taken place. Instead, things will get much worse because now you will have people trying to profit off those who have suffered tragedy at the hands of whatever giant beast just got done tearing the world appear.

One of the first opportunists trying to cash in will be insurance companies. These companies will now work to try covering losses from the damages after giant monsters attack, insisting they are willing to reimburse you for any damages that will take place during the next unfortunate GME. As there will be a plethora of these groups out there, you will have to make sure you don't just rush into anything drastic. Watch out for scammers and compare rates before you do any type of signing. You need to look for the insurance company that is willing to cover you no matter what kind of monster destroys your place. You don't want to have your house destroyed by some radioactive crawfish only to find out you only had a plan covering seawater giant monsters and not freshwater ones. Always make sure to read the fine print.

Charities

Other organizations that will be working to make a quick buck are "Monster Relief Aid" charities that hope they will be able to pull on your heartstrings. Yes, many of these causes will be legitimate and acting in the good of the community, but you have to make sure you are giving money to the right people and not some scam artist. It's best to question the people asking for the money for specifics on what they are doing with the money. If they are on the level, then you might want to think about helping out yourself. The best charities will be ones working to try to rebuild the homes of GME victims and help them to return to their normal way of life (at least as normal it can be now that the possibility of a creature the size of a skyscraper appearing out of nowhere and going on a destructive stroll through the city could be a daily occurrence).

That should be everything you need to know to help you survive when a giant monster attacks your city. Just to be on the safe side, here are couple reminders to keep you on track.

Be alert. Watch for warning signs that a giant monster might appear in the near future. When you can recognize that something is wrong, you are able to react to it more easily.

Be prepared. Now that you have read possible circumstances that might take place involving giant monsters, you'll be able to properly prepare yourself for when a GME occurs. Look over the different possible monsters and find the ones which you think are more likely to give you problems. That way, you'll be able to be ready when the monsters do show up.

Don't panic and use your wits. Remember that you will have to remain calm, as others around you will not. Don't point at the giant monster. Keep moving to make sure that you are able to make it to safety so that you can begin your counterattack. Unless you have enough equipment to properly fend off a giant monster, you'll want to make sure that you escape before you think about attacking it.

Keep this book handy. No one expects you to memorize

this book after your first reading, and there'll probably be some points that you have missed or forgotten. Keep a copy of this book around just to refresh yourself and even consider an additional copy to be kept with the giant monster supplies that you have been storing up. That way, you do not have to look around through the clutter of everyday life when you are under attack and instead just grab the stockpile of equipment you have tucked away. Everything should be together and ready at a moment's notice.

Keep these tips in mind and you will be able to overcome any obstacle that a GME can present. Thank you again for purchasing the Handbook for Surviving a Giant Monster Attack. The knowledge and wisdom you have learned helps to pay for itself. Have an uneventful day.

www.ingramcontent.com/pod-product-compliance
Lightning Source LLC
Chambersburg PA
CBHW032003170626
46807CB00006B/2625